BAD BLOOD

JANE BRITTAN

BLOWFISH BOOKS

BLOWFISH BOOKS

First published in Great Britain in 2016
by Blowfish Books
Blowfish Books Ltd,
15 Bennerley Road,
London SW11 6DR
www.blowfishbooks.com

ISBN: 978-0-9932334-3-2

Also available as an ebook
Mobi ISBN: 978-0-9932334-4-9
Epub ISBN: 978-0-9932334-5-6

A catalogue record for this book is available
from the British Library.

Typeset by Chandler Book Design

Printed and bound by
Booksfactory Print Group Sp. z o.o. Poland

For my father

1

September 2013

Did you ever try holding your breath? See how long you could do it for? Time yourself? Feel your chest fill up, the tubes under your skin closed and boiling, feel your fingers go numb as you watch the second hand pitch and crawl?

I'm doing it now.

Wet grass and tarmac and Sam's whining about nothing. I'm squeezing my eyes half shut and I can see the light catching in the spray from someone's football.

Holding my breath.

He's got some beef about a teacher. 'I told him I'm not doing it. In his dreams am I doing that. Prick. First day back and he's in to me …'

I let it go slowly. 'Yeah.'

'Well?'

'Well, what?' I scan the yard: it's spitting rain.

The kids with the football are packing up.

'Well,' he drags out the 'well'. 'What do you think?'

I look at him: collar up, pokey nose, angry rash on his chin. I say, 'Sounds like you did the right thing.'

He shrugs his shoulders, leans forward and slaps me on the back. 'Cool.'

The bell starts droning then and from every door bodies pour out and push towards the gates. We walk out together and I pull out my papers and roll us both a cigarette.

'You doing anything later?' he says. '*Call of Duty*?'

'Yeah,' I say, flat. 'Come round mine.'

He stops and looks at me. 'What is it?'

'What's what?' I say.

'You seem a bit – I dunno – *off*.'

He's right. 'First day back,' I say. 'Shit summer – all that.'

'Oh,' he says, 'yeah,' waits. 'Yeah, of course. Yeah.' Takes a breath and says in a rush, 'Mine wasn't all that either.'

Now I happen to know he spent most of the summer at his cousins' place in the south of France and I also happen to know he got himself well and truly laid by a friend of theirs; so there's shit and there's shit, and there's his summer. Still, Sam's all right. He's a mate. We walk up to the London Road then he goes his way.

'See you later,' he says and turns and kicks off down the road. He always walks right on the kerb like a gymnast on the high beam. Never seen anyone over the age of four do that.

I walk back through the park. It's light but the sky's heavy – it's got that grey sheen in it like it's going to pour down.

Karen's car is in the drive. I can hear the hoover wheezing from the sitting room. I creep in and I'm half way up the stairs when Charlie comes out of his room.

'Whoa!' he says, 'what's up? Where were you?'

I look at him. He's serious. 'School started today.'

'School? We still doing that?'

'Piss off,' I say and go to my room. He follows me and stands in the doorway. I squat down to get at my games but I can feel he's behind me, not moving. I look back at him, then I really look. 'What are you wearing?'

'What?' There's a kind of smirk on his face.

'That.'

'Taking it with me.'

I swallow. I don't even know why it's choking me to see him in it. 'Why?' I say because I can't think of anything else to say.

'We need something smart – a jacket. I didn't have one and it's no good asking you and … Karen didn't see a problem with it. It's just hanging there.' He trails off a bit. I'm still staring at him. 'What's the big deal?' he says.

'There isn't one. I just … nothing.'

Then he comes out with it: 'He'd have wanted –'

I get up, walk over, shove him out the door and slam it so it rattles. 'Don't,' I whisper after him.

I hear his feet on the landing and a soft whistle.

I close my hands into fists and I stand there, and the room spins around me. I don't know how long after it is but there's a faint knock on the door and I watch the handle turn.

'Ben?' It's Karen. She's been listening of course. 'Come and have some supper?' She says it gently, the way you'd coax a small child off a window ledge.

'Not hungry, thanks,' I say.

'Just a bite?' she says. 'It's chicken.'

I can either stay here and listen to her wheedling or go and eat. 'OK.'

Charlie's at the table, still wearing the jacket. There's a thread pulled loose on the cuff. I remember it – I don't even know why.

'Here he is!' he says, smiling, lifting a forkful of food to his mouth. 'Come on Benny.'

I sit down. 'Piss off,' I breathe.

Karen sits, then stands up, then sits down again. She hacks me off a chicken leg, biting her bottom lip. 'Beans?'

I'm still looking at Charlie. 'No thanks.'

'So,' she starts, 'how was school?'

But she doesn't get an answer because Charlie says, 'Listen Ben, what is it with you? Is it the jacket? Is it really about this?' He throws down his fork and starts taking it off. 'D'*you* want it? Is that it? You had your eye on it, did you?'

I sit quietly, squeezing my knife and fork.

'*What the fuck?*' he says.

'*Charlie,*' whispers Karen, 'Ben's very …'

'Very *what*?' I say. '*What am I*?'

She looks from him to me. 'Sad,' she says flatly. She pushes her plate away and leaves the table, switching on the overhead light on her way out. Suddenly there's a hundred watt of yellow light between us. And the word *sad* humming there like an echo.

Charlie rests his chin in his hands, breathes out. 'Listen mate. If you don't want me to wear it –'

'It's not that. It just – I don't know – it surprised me that's all. Take it.'

He sits back, his eyes still on me. 'How *was* school then?'

'Crap.'

'Sam still there?'

'Course. He's not going anywhere.'

'His brother said he had a girlfriend. This the same guy?'

I smile. 'Apparently.'

'Does he look any different? Spots cleared up?' He's helping himself to more chicken. I can hear Karen scratching at something in the kitchen.

'Nope.'

'Anyone new there this term?'

'What do you mean?'

'Duh.' He raises his eyebrows.

'Girls? Just leave it.'

He leans back, tipping his chair: 'Just saying.' He hitches the jacket back on and we get up to clear the table.

Later, after Karen's gone and Charlie's out, and I'm still waiting for Sam to turn up, I open the door to his study and straight away I can smell him.

2

Sam's late the next morning and I don't wait. I get to the gates at quarter to nine. When I get there, I hang back and the machinery in my head starts up like it always does. I start thinking about what's happened and what's next and why I ever thought about going back to school – like this was in any way a good idea. I lost whatever it was a long time ago. Last term, before my exams, after it all went wrong, I couldn't see straight anymore. I could see the words on the page but they just fused into the paper, so that Mrs Hughes' worksheet on *The Mayor of Casterbridge* just looked like fuzzy felt, and anything I tried to write came out like a load of demented spiders.

I'm deep in all of that – just mashing about in it up to my waist – when Sam rolls up.

'You never waited.'

'You were late.'

'So are you now. What you doing out here?'

I look across the yard and it's empty. In every window, there are dark silhouettes of teachers teaching. 'God.'

'What?' he says as we career towards the entrance.

'See you later,' I say and I'm on the stairs before he can ask me anything else.

'Ben, is it? You're late,' says Sir, new teacher, six inches shorter than me and trying to grow a beard. 'Second day in – poor start I'd say, wouldn't you?'

Everyone turns to look at me.

I nod.

'Sit down.'

I don't even look. I pile my bag on the table and sit in the seat nearest the door. He's reading out names and classrooms and telling us stuff, and all of it – all the noise – settles into a kind of low burr. I look over at the window – banks of clouds rolling, and far away, the hum of traffic up on the London Road. Slowly, very slowly I pull myself back into the room, mainly because someone's elbow's digging into my arm.

'Sorry, but …' I hear. I turn and it's like a punch or a lightning bolt and for a moment I forget about everything else.

She's slim, with red hair tied in a plait down her back and dark, clear blue eyes, and there's a kind of warm off her like a light that's been left on.

I've never seen her before.

She's sitting hunched against the wall because I'm taking up most of the table space. Of course I don't realise that until she says, 'Can you move your stuff?'

I swallow and nod like an idiot. 'Sorry. Sorry.'

I sweep my bag off the table, taking with it her ring binder which bursts open scattering file paper and those coloured subject-divider things. 'Sorry,' I say again and all I've said to her is 'sorry', and now Sir's telling everyone to move and go to the hall.

She looks like she's about to burst into tears.

I get up, kick back the chair. People are filing out.

Will slides up, pushes me into her and says, 'Wanker,' then shoots off into the corridor howling. The room empties and I'm still standing there, watching her on the floor grabbing her papers.

I don't know what to do. 'Shall I …? Do you need any help?' I say, and she looks up at me. There are faint freckles over her nose like they've been painted on.

I get down and help, and when she's packed it all up, she says, 'Thanks.' And goes out leaving the door squeaking slowly to a close.

I look for her in the hall but I don't see her. After the talk about the sixth form and the usual bullshit about responsibility and integrity and 'applying' ourselves, from the head teacher, we spill out and I find Sam. He's shrugged up against the fence on the field.

'All right?' he says.

I'm turning up a flint with my toe, prising it out of the ground. Then I see her. She's wearing a red coat and she's on her own. I nudge Sam. 'Who's that?'

He looks up, eyes swivelling. 'What? Who?'

I point. 'Red coat.'

He pushes off the fence. 'Nice. Don't know. The new ones are in today from other schools. There's a load of them in my class. Sixth-form tourists.' He looks at me then. 'Why?'

'I don't know. I just … she's in my class. I sat next to her.'

'Yeah? Good work, dude.'

'Wasn't deliberate.'

'No.'

'What's that mean?'

'Just 'no'. As in, no, you don't have the balls or the brains to check someone out, then go and sit with them. What did you say to her?'

'Nothing. Nothing till I knocked all her papers on the floor.'

He laughs. 'Twat. Hey, did I tell you about my holiday?'

So not ready to hear this again. 'I heard about it.'

'Oh yeah? Who from?'

I'm about to answer when he prods me in the ribs. 'Dude … *buddy*. Look sharp.'

From all the way across the field, she's coming. I pull up my hood and I watch her from under it: short skirt, long legs and a bright look on her face. I freeze. Sam's melting away. 'Later,' he says.

'Sam? Mate?' I call after him. A few girls are standing a little way off and looking sideways at us. She's smiling and she's still walking. It's like everything except us has speeded up and cantered off, and there's us and this: a wet field, cold feet and those blue eyes on me.

Sam's found a couple of mates and they're watching too. I can feel the cords in my throat tightening, hot sweat on my neck and my hands.

She reaches me and her breath smokes in the cold air.

'Hi,' she says, 'I'm Sophy.'

3

I clap my arms against my sides, not because I'm cold but for something to do. I'm tall and she's not, and I sort of sink back against the fence, then stand up again.

'Hi,' I say.

'So –' she starts but the bell hammers out over our heads and I pick up my bag.

'Got to go. See you later,' I say and force my way across the ground away from her, one foot over the other and because I'm not looking, because I'm not looking at anything, because my eyes are almost closed, I walk straight into a puddle, and all around me there's noise, kids moving in groups, talking, shouting, laughing.

'What was that?' Sam catches me up. 'What the hell? The look on her face – what are you like?' I walk on but he doesn't stop. 'What did you say to her?'

'Give it a rest, mate. I don't know. I didn't say anything. I just … I just left her there.'

He looks at me and this time he works it out.

He doesn't push it.

'OK. OK. Whatever. Your call. Do you want to play some C.O.D.? My mum's out. But then I guess …'

'What?'

'Well, I mean, you know … your house – it's probably easier for you. You know …'

I know he doesn't mean it. Not like that.

'Yeah,' I say, 'yeah, it is easier. Not tonight though.'

Back on the tarmac, I risk a look behind me and she's gone.

I'm doing Art and Design. They call it 'vocational'. I bailed on most of my exams last term and although Karen wrote letters and took me to meetings where I sat looking at my shoes while they talked about me, I ended up with this, and while they'd probably call it a consolation prize, I guess it's keeping me just the right side of sane at the moment.

I pitch up in the Art room five minutes late, sit down at the back and score gobs of dried paint off the table top with a palette knife till we're told to find a spot and draw what we see.

I grab a stool and a board and set up by the window where I can see down onto the square by the Science Block and the entrance. I dredge in a pot for some charcoal and let it bleed soot onto the paper.

I like drawing – I like art – I'm OK at it but it's more than that. I like being left alone, and sitting here right now, building something, watching it come together on the page feels all right for a moment. The radio's

playing in the background, the chat's died down, it's
pretty peaceful and that's good and bad at the same time:
good, because I'm not being asked questions about the
Hoover Dam or the ethnography of Brazil like last year
but bad, because he's in my head and when it's quiet like
this, it's always the same. It only takes a minute and then
I can see him: his face at the wheel. Collar and tie and
colourless eyes staring straight at me and through me.

Ticking.

Down below I see red. She's crossing the square – on
her own – and I feel bad all over again for having walked
away from her on the field. She stops a moment, roots
in her bag, pulls out her phone and reads it. There's so
much light in her – it's the only way I can describe it
– and like a fat moth, I'm hooked and circling.

Before I know it, I get down from the stool, say,
'Toilet,' to the teacher, and I run, trainers slapping on
the lino. I swing down one, two, flights of stairs and
bowl out of the entrance onto the square, just in time
to see her walking away.

'Hey!' I call, breathing hard. She slows down, turns
and her shoulders go up like a cat's.

'Oh. Hey.' Her face is blank.

I go up to her, swallowing, willing out the words.
'I'm sorry about this morning. I wasn't … you know.'

She shrugs, looks away. 'That's OK,' she says and
I know if I don't say something amazing in the next
thirty seconds, she'll be gone forever.

'I'm Ben. I'm … you're new?'

She chews her lip, looks at me. 'Yes. I'm new.' She starts to walk away and I blurt out because I've lost all dignity and – what did the head teacher say? – integrity: 'You're gorgeous.'

I don't wait. I don't even know if she's heard me. I run like I've thrown a grenade, and I go back and finish my sketch in silence, turning what's just happened over and over in my head like a hog on a spit.

Still. I'm kind of pleased I did something. I actually got off my arse and did something that wasn't nothing.

I do Art all morning, then I look for her at lunch and wait in the form class for registration. I sit at the same table with my fists on my knees and I wait but she doesn't turn up. I even ask Sir where she is but he just raises an eyebrow and asks why I want to know.

I'm free in the afternoon and I head to the park, sit on a bench and roll a smoke. It looks like it's going to rain again. My trainers are falling apart – another soaking and they'll disintegrate. I can feel a headache coming on.

When I get home there's no one in and I realise I've gone out without my keys. The sky darkens and the rain sets in.

The side door to the garage is open but I never go in there now. I sit on the front porch, shrug up my hoodie and try to keep warm. I don't have to wait long, because after about fifteen minutes, when the rain is pounding and my feet are numb, a car drives up.

It's a black Bentley with a little crest shaped like a

stag standing up on the bonnet. Two men get out and walk towards the door. One's middle-aged, with short grey stubbly hair and glasses. The other's younger and very tall. He holds an umbrella for the older one. They're both wearing long overcoats and really, really shiny lace ups. I always notice shoes. Comes of never really looking anyone in the eye I suppose. They stop when they see me.

The younger one says, 'Who are you?' He speaks with a whiny American accent. 'Is this your house?'

I nod and they look at each other.

The other one says, 'You must be Ben, I think. Do you mind if we come in for a minute?'

I look at him. My head's hurting, my feet are burning with cold and I'm hopping from one foot to the other to get the circulation back. The rain's getting worse. It's pooling around the porch and in the cracks in the drive.

'It's nothing to worry about,' he says. 'We just wanted to have a chat. No one's in trouble or anything. It's about your … father. We're from Rees. There are a few small anomalies surrounding his death we wanted to clear up, a few … loose ends. Is there somewhere we can …?' He stops for a minute then says, 'I understand it might be painful for you …'

Painful? I don't know about anyone else but when someone gets up in my face like he is, I have to move. It's like a boiling saucepan, building up, the steam pushing at the lid – everything frothing and churning underneath – and to keep the lid from coming off completely, I have to get away. I square up to him and elbow him in the chest so he tips back and falls against his friend. Then I run. The American's going after me but I hear the other one calling, 'Leave him!'

I run through the rain and when I duck into a bus shelter, I'm wet through and my teeth are chattering and I can't stop them. I'm doubled over to catch my breath and when I look up, I see the car pass. The American's driving and he catches my eye. He smiles and accelerates close up to the kerb, driving a sheet of dirty water up from the gutter at me.

I don't remember what I do after that. I guess I just wander in and out of shops trying to warm up until the rain stops, and then at around five o'clock, I go home.

Karen's there with her apron on, and the kitchen's full of steam. She always wears that apron – it's like a fucking nurse's outfit: something she puts on when she's doing good.

She looks me up and down, working her eyebrows. 'Look at you, you're soaking,' she says.

I pull off my jacket and there's a barely perceptible intake of breath as it leaves a little trail of drips on the lino. 'Never mind!' she says brightly. 'I'll wipe that up.'

I stand at the hall mirror and push my hair out of my eyes. I'm blinking water and she's standing right behind me with her head on one side.

I turn and fold my arms. 'What?'

'Nothing,' she says.

There's the sound of a key in the lock and Charlie comes in. His hair's shaved to the skin.

'What do you think?' he says.

'Jesus,' I breathe.

Karen says, 'Oh Charlie. You look like a real soldier. Doesn't he, Ben?'

'Marine,' he says. 'Marine.'

'Of course.' She smooths her hands down her apron, picks off a crust of something and rolls it between her fingers. 'Your supper's on the table,' she says. 'I can't stay. It's Ray's footie night. See you tomorrow guys.' She goes in for a hug but I freeze. I can't do that anymore. She steps back and I can see she's about to lose it.

I take a breath. 'I'm OK, Karen. Really.'

'Yes but ...' she sniffs.

'He's all right,' says Charlie. 'You go on. Thanks for supper.'

She stretches her mouth into a smile but her eyes are empty. I watch her go and look beyond her up the road to the woods where tall trees crowd and catch at the darkening sky. When I go back into the kitchen, Charlie's standing there with his shirt off.

'Check it out,' he says. Spanning his left shoulder just above the blade, and covered in Clingfilm, is a dark tattoo in copperplate writing: a name and two dates – a birth and a death. 'Yeah?' he says, watching me. 'Insane isn't it? Just did it on a whim when I got my hair cut.' I know he's expecting me to switch, to lose it but I don't.

I say, 'Cool. Looks good.'

'He'd have hated it.'

'I don't know. Maybe. Don't know if he'd have been

that bothered.' I bend and pull the oven door open. He's putting on his shirt when I remember. 'What's an anomaly?'

'An anomaly?' He rolls his shoulders. 'Er ... something odd – out of place, something that doesn't fit. Why?'

I tell him about the car with the crest and the men.

He stares at me. 'Mate, I'm telling you, you don't want anything to do with them. It's enough. We've all had enough. You don't want that lot anywhere near you.'

'Why not?'

'Because,' he says, 'just because. Because we're moving on. *Aren't we?*' and I wonder whether he's trying to convince himself. 'I thought we talked about it.'

'No. *You* talked about it.'

We're eating in silence, leaning against the sink, when he stops and turns to me and says, 'Listen,' he seems awkward somehow. 'Are you going to be OK when I go?' It's so quiet, even the air is quiet, holding its breath.

'Yeah,' I say quickly. 'Yeah. Course.'

'I saw Maurice.'

'Oh yeah?'

'In the shop. He asked after you.'

'I'll go in soon.'

'Whatever mate,' he says with a smile. 'I've got shit to do.'

When I look at my phone later, there's an email. I never get personal emails and I'm about to delete it when I notice the address: @rees.

Dear Ben,

Please excuse me contacting you this way. I must
first apologise for what happened this afternoon. It
certainly wasn't my intention to shock or upset you.

Your father was a highly regarded member of staff
here at Rees. Without his tireless work I am sure
we would not have the international reputation we
are so proud of today. That is why I would like to
invite you to visit us to discuss not only his work, his
legacy, but also perhaps ways in which we may help
you going forward.

Can I suggest Friday at ten if that is convenient
for you?

Kind regards
Evan Greenhalgh

Below the message is a number and directions to
the place.

I don't say anything to Charlie. He's upstairs packing,
talking on his phone.

I'm in the study – *his* study – looking out of the
window, leaning where he used to lean.

The rain has stopped but fat drops are still knocking
off the porch roof onto the path. There's a skin of cloud
stretched across the sky and the moon like a fingernail
behind it.

Fuck.

4

In morning registration, before Sir's in, she's sitting there with her bag on her knees but there's someone next to her.

'Ed,' I say. He's chatting to her in that easy way he has – all the A1 body language, all the moves. What she won't know is, he's always doing it: it's like a game with him – any girl, anywhere – and if they don't put out first time, he'll move on.

He looks up, annoyed. 'What?'

She's watching.

'I'm sitting there,' I say, 'you're in my seat.'

'*You what?*'

I swallow bile. I want to hit him. Other people are watching us now.

'Just …' I say. He stands up, folds his arms. I'm not scared of him. I'm bigger than him. I know I can take him but there's something in her eyes that makes me not want to.

Then she says to him, 'Actually, he was sitting there yesterday.'

He turns to look at her. 'Whatever,' he says, and to me, but still looking at her, 'Dozy slut. Wouldn't bother if I was you. Might catch something.'

I ram him against the wall and I spend the rest of the day in Isolation with a warning.

After school, I go to the park and sit down on a bench near the kids' playground. It's been raining again and there's a bright steam off the paths. The place is empty – silent – except for hissing and dripping from the lines of trees.

I breathe in and out, sucking in the cold clear air, trying to think. Trying to think about what going into Rees would be like. I sit back on the bench and look around me. A figure in the distance is coming my way and as it gets closer, I see with a jolt, it's her, walking down the path, swinging her bag. She's on her own.

I shrink back into the seat and feel her walk by, sure she hasn't seen me but then I hear her stop a few feet past my bench. I look up and she's turned and she's smiling at me like she knew I was there all along. Something about that makes me angry. But I don't get up and go. Instead, I scramble in my pocket for my papers.

'Hey,' she says. She sits next to me on the wet bench.

'Hi,' I mutter into my lap.

'You OK?'

I rub my hands in my hair. 'Yeah. Yeah.'

'Um,' she starts, 'that's never happened to me before.'

I fumble with my matches and light up. 'What?'

'Someone … sticking up for me. Unless, well … maybe you didn't – maybe it was about something else but –'

I shake my head and look down. But I can't not look at her for long. 'No. It was … I mean … it was about you. He's a prick. I shouldn't have done it, but –'

'Well,' she says, 'maybe not.' She smiles. 'But then, apart from you, he's about the only person who's spoken to me since I got here.' She pauses. 'I used to go to The Marist, the Convent school. I hated it, we had regulation gloves and hats – all that crap. So I wanted a change for the Sixth Form. But it's hard to make friends when everyone's known each other for years. It's hard to … Christ … I'm just babbling. Sorry.'

I smile then, a bit. 'No. No …' I say, 'you're all right.'

'You don't mind?'

I shake my head. 'No.'

'So where do you live?' she says.

'Twyford Close, up near the London Road, by the woods.'

She nods, then waits, then flicks a look at me. 'I heard that –'

'My dad?'

Then she says, 'Busted. None of my business, I'm really sorry. I heard –'

'Right.'

'Sorry.'

'That's OK.'

'When did he –?'

'May,' I say quickly and just when I'm about to ask her a question so I can forget about him for five minutes, she looks at me and says quietly, 'I'm sorry.'

I ball up like a spring. Here I am with the one person I actually want to talk to and there's the one thing – the *one* thing – I do *not* want to have a conversation about, and here we are having it.

She's not giving up. She says, 'So, you live with your Mum?'

'She died when I was eleven.'

'Oh.'

I look at the floor because I know what's coming. Pity – like a fucking express train – another thing I don't want.

'So, who looks after –?'

'I'm OK. We're OK. I'm with my brother, my older brother. And … my aunt looks after us – makes sure we're not dealing crack or leaving the toilet seat up. I –' I swallow, and say more quickly than I intend, 'What about you?'

'I live on Bedford Road, number 45. I live with my parents and my little sister. I'm doing English and Geography and French and … um … I play guitar. I don't know: what else?'

I watch her face and its lights and darks; then she stops and says, 'So, your dad …?'

I say it, and I don't know how I do, but when I've

said it, I feel my throat loosening for the first time in forever. 'Suicide.'

'That's awful. God, Ben.'

And then I find myself saying, 'I found him'

'Christ.'

And there it is. Just what you don't want to happen when you're sitting with the most beautiful girl you've ever met, and she's listening to you and you want to touch her and kiss her. There it is: I'm crying. I push my hands into my eye sockets to stop the flow. But I can't staunch it: the missing him and what I couldn't say to him – all of it – it's like blood from a deep cut and it just keeps coming. But when I look at her through my tears, I see she's at it too.

She says, 'Ben … it's OK, it's OK to be sad. It's OK.'

I give a muffled response and I find myself remembering a Sunday lunch – years ago – roast whatever-it-was and Dad is carving like he's removing a spinal tumour, and I'm telling Charlie a joke I heard, and Dad puts down the knife carefully – he always did everything carefully – and listens, really leans in and listens, and it's a stupid joke about nothing and he doesn't get it, and we have to explain it to him, and he's asking questions and he's trying to understand and he's so fucking clever but he doesn't get it. He never did.

But he laughed anyway. That kills me.

Sophy puts her arm round my shoulder and rubs my back. It's a bit Head Prefect rather than potential girlfriend but it feels OK. I feel better for having told

someone. She reaches out her hand and brushes her
thumb gently across my cheek.

I want to kiss her, really want to. And then she kisses
me. Just a peck like you'd comfort a small child really
but she smells so good – her hair's wet with the rain
and it smells of fruit. A strand of it sticks against my
cheek for a moment and I can feel it on my skin for
ages after. Then there's more back rubbing. Then just
when I think I might try it for real, her phone goes
and she checks it.

'Look, I have to go. I'm sorry.'

I nod, wipe my face on my sleeve. I sit back on the
bench like I'm ready to spend the night out there with
the squirrels. She gets up to go and her phone falls on
the damp ground. We both lean down to get it but I
get there first.

'Give me your number?' she says.

I stand up. I punch in my number and she looks up
at me with a broad smile. 'See you at school.'

She says it like it's a question.

She starts walking, and I watch her go, then she stops
suddenly and paces back. 'If you ever want to … if you
ever need a friend,' she looks down, whispers, 'because
… I know I do.' She rests the flat of her hand against
my arm. 'I mean it,' she says. Then she's gone.

It's getting dark and I'm freezing. I get up and walk
home with the trees rustling over me like laughing.

When I get in, the house is empty and there's an
envelope on the mat with my name on it.

I turn it over in my hands. Once. Twice. A small cream envelope and my name in blotchy capitals in green ink.

I don't open it straightaway.

I take it into the study, into the quiet and I breathe him in again. I sit at his desk. It belonged to his father. It's old, pitted and marked all over with ancient ink stains and it has brass key plates and handles. There are drawers on the bottom and a top bit under the sloping lid that has little compartments with tiny wooden knobs. On the top of the desk, there's a photograph of him, the one when he got his PhD, in his robes, with a kind of faraway look in his eyes.

I look around the room. There's stuff everywhere: papers, notebooks, box files, their lids pulled shut with twine. His ID card for work still hangs from a nail on the wall and his picture, unsmiling and fuzzy, stares out at me. Glass containers of dried insects and fungus are ranged unsteadily on shelves under a fine coating of dust.

And all around the walls hang his pictures: a collection of creepy black and white Victorian illustrations. I lean forward and straighten one: a shadowy engraving, heavily cross-hatched and shaded. It shows a man in a long robe turning back to look at me.

This room is still full of him – like spores, like dust, like tiny particles of glass.

I put my hand on the envelope, span it, cover it. Very slowly I open it, sheer along the top with my finger, feel the stiffness, the crackle; pinch out a sheet of paper. It's folded in four and I open it up on the desk. Three lines, also in green:

TRUST NO ONE.
TELL NO ONE.
FIND THE RED GULL.

5

I cross to the window and look out: the road's empty. On the hill beyond the trees, a fox stands stock still in the moonlight.

Find the Red Gull. What is the Red Gull? I hammer and jar at my memory but there's nothing. I have no idea what it could mean.

Charlie's at his girlfriend's. I know he won't be back tonight and I know he won't want to answer me but I call him anyway. He takes a few moments to pick up, and all the while, the green ink on the paper glows.

'What's up?' he says, 'you OK?'

'Yeah, yeah.'

'What then?'

'Have you heard of the Red Gull?'

'The Red Gull? No. What's that? A pub or something?'

'Don't know. You sure?'

There's a pause and I can hear her voice behind

him. Then he says, 'Mate, are you actually serious?
You're calling me up to ask me this when I'm leaving
on Tuesday and I'm not going to see Ellie for weeks?'

'Yeah. No. Sorry.'

'Later.' A click and he's gone. Fair enough.

The Red Gull.

I sit down and Dad's old desk spreads itself out in
front of me.

I tug on a brass handle and open a drawer. It's full
of papers. Some are rough workings out on graph
paper: equations of some sort. It's weird to see his
handwriting again.

Underneath one of the drawers, there's a secret
cubby hole. He showed me once when I was little. Mum
was out and Charlie had upset me. I don't remember
why. I went into the study where Dad was sitting,
crooked over his desk and he turned to see me sniffing.
He never did what normal adults do when a kid's crying
but it didn't matter because he was good anyway. He
hoisted me carefully onto the end of his knee and, with
ink-stained fingers, he opened every drawer in the desk
slowly and talked to me about what he kept in there.

The cubby hole is in one of the tiny drawers in the
top section on the left. I remember that you have to push
the drawer in twice and then pull it out. Underneath is
a little cavity, about 4 cm deep and 10 cm wide and all
that's in there is a torn newspaper cutting. The top bit's
gone so I can't see the date. On one side, there's half
of an ad for a car, on the other, a small column feature:

'Mystery Illness in French Town: Brit
holidaymakers caught up in outbreak – public
health officials insist there is no need for concern
and local reports suggest that contaminated flour
from local mills is the likely source ...'

I stare at it, read it over and over but there's nothing
more – just some random news story. I scratch around in
the hole for anything else but there's nothing. I screw up
the paper, pitch it into the bin and sit back where I was.

Dad was brilliant. You've got no idea.

Weird.

But brilliant.

He was a scientist. He'd worked for Rees, this giant
pharmaceutical company, for years. I don't know what
he did. Wasn't interested. It wasn't like he was Mick
Jagger or anything – he just did this normal, run-of-
the-mill, 9 to 5 job. He wore a suit and a tie, carried a
briefcase, caught the 7.45am train into Farnham every
morning, went to his allotment and dug potatoes on a
Sunday. He liked timetables and counting, and baked
beans with everything, hated the colour yellow, but
most of all he liked things to be the same. Always:
routine, rituals – it was compulsive.

He did do stuff with us, not like normal Dads – park
and football stuff – but stuff he liked. He was interested
in insects, knew everything about them. We spent a
lot of time looking for them and at them and inside
them – cutting bits off them, drawing them, that sort
of thing. But I liked it – I liked listening to him talk.

He never looked right at you. He'd fix his eyes on the wall or the ceiling and rattle on for hours.

Soon after Mum got ill, he went to a conference in France – a work thing – and he brought back an old-fashioned doctor's box he'd bought in an antique shop. It was made of cherry wood and it stood tall: about a foot high, and when you opened the top, the front would flip down. It had little polished drawers and racks to hold the equipment. There were bottles in coloured glass, a stethoscope with fleshy rubber tubing and on the lower level, a row of glass syringes arranged in size order. The glass on the plungers was decorated in swirls of gold and green and the handles of the plunger were elaborate and delicate, also in gold, and they curled around like the handles of scissors.

One day, when Mum was resting upstairs and I was playing outside with Charlie, he called me in. He had a syringe in his hand.

He took me into his study and sat me on his desk. He said he needed my help, said it was for an experiment, that it might help Mum get better and that I had to be brave. Very gently, he rolled up my sleeve and pushed the needle into the crook of my arm. I watched as my blood smoked back under the patterned glass. Afterwards, he said very solemnly, 'Thank you, Ben.'

It happened quite a lot after that: taking blood – sometimes with Charlie too but mostly with me. I sort of looked forward to it. He said we were 'making science' together.

It didn't help though, whatever he was doing. Mum got worse and then better and then much worse and then it was hopeless.

He was always working then. Weekends he spent in his study, scratching out spidery chemical formulae on endless sheets of paper that he'd stick up around the walls or line up in rows on the floor. I'd see him in the mornings, his face white and lined, and his eyes burning in his head.

And after she died, when none of us could see straight, he asked me again – just me this time – my blood. Wordless, methodical: taking my blood, injecting me – over and over – and I let him because I saw how much it mattered to him, that it meant something.

I can still see the marks: tiny red tracks and blots in the crook of my arm.

Traces of him under my skin.

6

The next day I've got a free morning so I head to the Mall to see Maurice. He runs the Games Workshop and he's done it forever. Charlie and I used to be into it big time: collecting the figures, doing all the painting. It seems lame now I suppose – not that being cool is really at the top of my list of priorities at the moment – but playing imaginary battles and painting toys at seventeen: I wouldn't exactly be helping myself.

Maurice is around forty and he's a major gamer. I'm not sure that in a *real* battle against other actual human beings with swords and shit, Maurice would really cut it. He's a paunchy dude. Mostly he wears an ACDC T-shirt under a knitted tank top and they're both too small for him. If you look and believe me, it's not a sight you'll get over in a hurry, you'll see his white hairy belly pushing out underneath them, just above his belt.

But in *Throne of Skulls* or *Island of Blood*, Maurice is your man. Maurice has got it going on. I like Maurice.

He's a mate. He doesn't judge me; he doesn't patronise me. He talks to me about *White Dwarf* and all that and sometimes, when the shop's quiet, he says, 'You all right? No school today?' I know he's not looking to fix me or change me. He's just being nice. And that makes a big difference.

When I get to the shop, he's leaning on a scale model of Helm's Deep, chatting to another gamer called Bernie who's always at the shop. They met in the virtual world game, Second Life. By all accounts, Bernie's avatar is pretty fit: he's got wings and scales and a kind of devil tail. In real life, objectively, I'd say Bernie's not got a lot going for him

Anyway, I hang around watching people come and go, till Maurice finishes with Bernie and comes over.

He's rubbing his hands together. 'Wow! Bernie's on a roll: Lizardman Stegadon and two battalions! One hundred and fifty buckaroos, thank you very much! Things are looking up!' then after a pause, 'You all right? Come round the back and have a cuppa. Aren't you cold in that? Jim, keep an eye out for me, will you?'

A man dressed from head to toe in purple camouflage looks up and nods.

The back of the shop is a mess. Boxes of kit and paints lie all over the place. Some opened, some still in their cellophane. There's an old TV and a PlayStation 2. At the back of the little room is a stained sofa with a broken arm. It's covered in piles of gaming mags. Maurice's desk has a laptop, a microwave with a pot noodle still inside from the last time I was here, at least three bits of sandwich in different stages of decay and a Lord of the Rings thermos.

He shuffles about, filling the kettle from a grubby sink in the corner.

'Park yourself, amigo,' he says, moving the mags onto the floor and I sink into the sofa. Most of the seat is kind of spiny but it has a Maurice-shaped dent in it and if you find that, you're all right.

'So, what's new in the zoo?' he says. I shrug and pick up a magazine dated June 2001.

He turns to his desk and opens a drawer. 'Biscuit?' He says it like it's French: *Bisquwee.'*

I take two. 'Nothing much,' I say. 'School's started.'

'Oh yeah?'

I say it quickly: 'Maurice, have you heard of something called the Red Gull?'

He thinks about it, scratches his balls and says, 'No mate. What is it?'

I shrug. 'Nothing. Just something I heard about.'

'Right.' There's a pause – not awkward, just a space – then he says, 'Yeah,' like we're in the middle of a long conversation, 'business is cracking at the moment. We had a *lady* in here last week. Now we have not had that in a while. They tend to order online. Nice. Nice to have a change … makes a change.'

He dries up then and goes and makes the tea. I don't look like the best listener in the world. I don't say much, I don't make all the little nods and hums that tell you to keep going which is ironic really because I am the best listener in the world. I'm really, really good at it. I spend my life listening. When the tea's done, he leans forward with the ginger-nuts and says, 'You doing much at the moment?'

I look at him. He could have been talking about anything: dry-stone walling, stamp collecting, masturbating. But he isn't. He's talking about gaming.

'Not so much.'

He nods wisely. That's the thing with Maurice. He doesn't go on. No follow-up questions about how you *feel* about it all. I've had it with feelings.

Then out of the blue he says, 'Got a girlfriend?'

'Maurice. I – er, what the –?'

He nods slowly and coughs. 'I might have one.'

There's a silence and we look at each other then both look away. 'Yeah. Yeah. It's not definite. But the vibes are good man. Rinky-dinky, mate!'

I've no idea what 'rinky-dinky' is even supposed to mean but I make the thumbs-up sign at him and stare into my tea. 'Nice.'

'I know,' he says. 'She's called Jo. Works in Greggs. I get my lunch in there. They do a heat up in the shop for you. I go in for the pasties. Nice and toasty. They heat them up for you. I just started chatting one day when I was waiting for the microwave. She lives near me; would you believe it?'

'Good for you,' I say.

'Tops, isn't it?' he says. 'Yesterday, I got caught up

with a big order, so I'm late for lunch right? *Bloodcrushers of Khorne*: full Monty. Bloke's come all the way from *Walthamstow*. Anyway, I get in and what do you think? She's only saved the last pasty for me. Saved it. For me. So we got chatting, like I said, and I told her where I work. She's only on Second Life, isn't she? We're meeting up tonight.'

'Sounds like you're in there, mate.'

He settles back and picks a few crumbs off his chest. 'Well. It's only a virtual date at the mo. On the Grid. Just taking it slow. Women are tricky beasts, Ben.'

I nod and stand up to go. 'You off then?' he says.

'Yeah. You know me: places to be, people to see.'

Maurice makes the Vulcan sign of peace and turns back to his ginger-nuts.

Right. So even Maurice has a girlfriend. Well, a sort of a one. I go past Greggs on the way out of the Mall and look in. Sure enough, there she is. Frizzy red hair and arms like a trucker. She has a nice smile.

In the back pocket of my jeans is the note about the Red Gull, about not telling anyone.

But what I want to know is – what am I not telling anyone? What is there that *I* know that I should be keeping from the rest of the human race? I go round and round it till my brain is frying. I make up my mind then and there though, that, number one, I *am* going to Rees tomorrow, and two, I'm going to ask Sophy out.

Going to school is like falling head first into a great open mouth: you spend hours thrashing and flailing about in a wet gullet until at three o'clock, it coughs and hocks and spits you out again. I wait at the grille gates at the South end, trying to look like I'm not looking for someone. I fold and unfold my arms, I walk up and down a bit, and kids of all shapes and sizes rub and chatter and shuffle past me. I've been there twenty-five minutes when finally, I clock her.

Seeing her jolts me. I stand there for a second, just staring, waiting for whatever arthritic rodent is working the controls in my brain to switch me on and propel me in her direction. It doesn't happen and I find it's put me into reverse and I'm actually walking away, head down, chewing the inside of my lip.

That is, until I hear her. 'Ben! Hey! Ben?'

I turn slowly, chimpanzee grin on my face. 'Hi.'

'I thought you saw me. Were you waiting for someone?'

'No.'

'Oh. OK.'

She waits, swinging her bag against her knees, and I'm looking at her out of the corner of my eye. 'So ...' she says.

'I best be –' I start.

But she jumps in, breathless. 'You want to come back to mine?'

I stare at her. 'Yeah. Yes. That'd be great.' I turn and walk along with her. But what I'm walking into and what I'm going to do when I get there, I have no idea.

At her house, she goes up to the door with her keys,

and I follow her very slowly. When I look up, she's standing on the doorstep looking back at me and she's so beautiful it actually makes my stomach turn over.

'Are you OK?' she says.

I swallow. 'Yeah.'

'You coming in? Mum! It's a friend from school. We're just going upstairs.'

I haven't really been into any girls' bedrooms since I was about twelve. It's nice: full of photos, lots of postcards and pictures cut out of magazines. She has a double bed with a white cover on it and coloured cushions.

She moves a towel and some clothes off the bed, and I sit down on one of her bras. I leap up, grab it from under me and give it to her. That feeling of lace and wire stays with me for hours after. She leans forward and looks at me. 'You want a coffee? Something to eat? I can –'

'Nah. It's fine. I'm good. Thanks. Nice room.'

'Thanks.' She's still moving around, putting stuff away. She sits down next to me after a bit and undoes her hair, shakes it out, then pulls it up into a handful and lets it fall. I watch her transfixed, my head spinning. And as she talks about nothing in particular, more than anything in the world I want to kiss her.

Then she notices that I've kind of dropped out of the programme and she says again, 'Are you sure you're OK?'

I have to come up with something so it looks like I was thinking about something important. I reach into my pocket and pull out the paper about the Red Gull.

'What is it?' she says.

'No idea. It was pushed through my letter box.'

'That's so weird.' She takes it, turns it over, then hands it back to me.

Our fingers are almost touching. I'm watching her and her lips are full, and time crawls as I lean in just a fraction and our breath knits up in the air between us, and then it all comes to an abrupt end, as the man I guess is her dad appears in the doorway and just stands there looking at me. He's the biggest man I've ever seen and he's got the look of an angry silverback gorilla. I get up to go and she follows me down.

At the door she says, 'Never mind about him.' I'm about to say something when she says, 'I've got a half day tomorrow. If you want to hang out … I mean –' She looks up at me, biting her bottom lip.

'Yeah. Yeah, I would.'

I go out onto the street where headlights burn in puddles, and I hear my feet on the road and my heart in my chest. And her voice in my head.

7

Karen's outside on the landing with the hoover at seven o'clock.

She's got her earphones in and she's singing tune-lessly as the nozzle bats up against the skirting.

I make toast and eat it on the way to the station.

I get into Farnham at about quarter to ten and get a bus to Rees. The first thing I see is the sign in massive green capitals: REES GLOBAL. And under the name, a stag like the one on the car.

The main buildings are surrounded on all sides by high fencing and there's a security box at the gate. After a phone call the guys wave me through but they look mean. I go in through giant glass revolving doors and up to the reception desk where two women sit. Behind them is a huge board with the names of different departments. One of the women, Asian, with very short hair and a name badge that says she's called Mayumi, stands up when I walk in.

'Can I help you?' She has an American accent.

I ask for Evan Greenhalgh and she says, 'Oh yes.' She makes a call, then: 'OK. Just take a seat and someone will come collect you.'

I go and sit some distance away from her on a large black and steel sofa and watch people coming and going. They all wear ID cards around their necks, with their pictures on, like the one in Dad's study. They're all in suits and they all look like they think they're pretty damn important – like if they were off work with a cold one day, the sun would fall out of the sky and all the crops would fail – you know the sort of look. I think about Dad and I wonder if he had that look at work. Maybe he did but then I don't know if he'd have cared that much about looking the part.

Change is hard for most people but I think for Dad it was like being run over again and again by a fire truck. Mum dying was shit for all of us. It was toxic and sad and even though we all knew it was coming, when it happened, it broke us. But when you're a kid, you can sort of put stuff back together. You can. But Dad, I think he was broken so badly, he never got over it.

He kind of checked out. He spent long hours in his study with the door locked. He still sat down to meals with us, he was still weird about food, still didn't get people; in fact, the weirdness got worse, it took on a whole new dimension: he started buying stuff in bulk. The cellar was full of tins of food and boxes of soap

that we never used, it still is. He kept working of course
but something had gone out of him.

I grind my fingers into my eye sockets. When I look
up a woman is standing in front of me: Annie Rivers.
I know from her ID card. Annie Rivers looks like a
human seal. She has tight-fitting, shiny clothes that
squeak as she walks, short cropped hair, dark lipstick
and a man's watch.

'Hello.' She speaks in a husky rasp. 'Ben Collins?'

I get to my feet and shake the hand that's offered.
Damp and warm.

'I'm Annie, I'm Mr Greenhalgh's PA. Can you follow
me? He's waiting for you.'

Tell no one. Trust no one is going round in my head.
What am I doing here?

She takes me up in the lift, then across bridges, down
corridors, past rooms full of important-looking people
having important-looking meetings, then up again and
through a door with a swipe-key into a suite of rooms
with floor-to-ceiling windows and weird abstract art
on the walls. She knocks on a door and I hear her say,
'He's here.'

Someone says something but I don't catch it. She
gestures to a chair near what turns out to be her desk.
'He won't be long, Ben.' She smiles.

The room smells of static. There's a bunch of flowers
on her desk and a spray of pollen dust underneath them.
She sits down, locks her fingers together, tips her head
on one side and looks at me. 'You're David's son?'

I look up. 'Yeah. Younger son.'

'You know, it's funny, until … well, I didn't know he had children. He didn't seem the type.'

'You knew him?'

'Mmm. Yes. He worked here in the Biotech arm. He was a very good scientist. Very … thorough. Passionate about his work. Driven. Until –' As she says it, she fixes me with an odd look and I can't make out what she means by it.

'Until what?'

There's a soft crunch and she looks up. The door to the inner office is opening. She leans in to me quickly and says, 'Be careful Ben.'

'What?'

But she's shaking her head, shuffling papers, getting up. 'Ah, Ben, this is Mr Greenhalgh, he's our Research Director.'

'Evan, *please*,' he says to me, taking my hand and squeezing hard. 'We've already met haven't we?'

There's a kind of buzz coming off him, like a coil of bright light that you can't quite see through.

I follow him into the room.

Inside, there's a vast leather desk, a sofa and a low table. Pink lights belly from the ceiling like udders and the world outside hums far below us.

'Thanks for coming in,' he says. 'I wasn't sure you'd got my email.'

'No. Sorry,' I say, 'I should've …' We look at each other. Folds of flesh bag under his eyes.

'No problem, no problem,' he says. 'How about a coffee?'

'No thanks.'

'Have a seat.' I sit on the sofa and fold my arms. I watch him as he leans back on his desk, picks up an elastic band and twines it around his fingers. 'Well,' he says, 'first off, I'm sorry about the other day. We didn't mean to startle you.'

I shrug and he waits, then says, 'How are you? How are you bearing up? I hear your brother's off to join the army, is it?'

'Marines,' I mutter. 'How did you know that?'

He comes and sits next to me on the sofa, crosses his legs.

'Maybe I didn't make it clear how very … special your father was. Well, no, that's not entirely true. I should really say – *on the record* – *all* our employees are special to us. But your father – David –' He stops and looks at me a moment. 'He was truly outstanding. I know you won't have known much about what he did. We have a very strict code of secrecy here, for obvious reasons. But what I can tell you, is that he was quite remarkable – a *genius*. We have a lot of very clever men and women working here but there are very few who would fall into that category. Which brings me back to your question: I know about your brother, partly because your father talked about him, about you too, before he died. And I know about you now, because we like to feel we're still connected, involved with our *families.* Does that make sense?' He leans in a little.

Trust no one. Tell no one.

'Yeah, I guess,' I say. 'So, what did you want to talk to me about?'

He eyes me a minute more, then straightens up again. 'OK. As I said, your father was a brilliant man but, like many of his kind, he was rather … disorganised. When he died, we did what we always do in these cases and conducted a thorough … er … audit of his work, his research archive. Now, we're fairly certain that he was onto something extremely important connected with his work on gene therapy in cancer but …' He smiles, sighs. 'We found it to be incomplete. In other words, what we were hoping to find wasn't there. Now, I know he worked from home a lot, I know he was very private about his work, so, we'd like to ask your permission to have a look through what he's got there, just in case. I can arrange for someone to come over at your convenience to take it away – you'll probably be glad of the space. I expect there's a lot of it, eh?'

I stare at him. 'And?'

'And what?'

'You said something about me. About helping me.'

'Yes. Yes, of course. Well, I wanted to talk about your future, what we can do for you, how we can help get you off the ground so to speak. I know things haven't been easy. There's a mentoring programme you might be interested in, we have contacts in banking and law… bursaries to fund –'

I want to throw up. I get to my feet.

'Ben?'

'I have to get back.'

He gets up too, hovering. That buzz again. 'Have I … I hope I haven't said the wrong thing?'

Now I'm just holding it together. 'I just remembered I have to be somewhere.'

'Yes … of course. But … your father's research papers? I wonder if we could arrange to –?'

'I don't know. I'll talk to my aunt.'

'Right. Right, of course.' He pulls out a wad of cards, snaps one out and hands it to me. 'Here's my card – personal email. Just let me know when's convenient.'

'Bye,' I say.

'I'll get Annie to walk you down.'

We shake hands, he opens the door and she's waiting.

On our own in the lift, I say, 'What did you mean when you said *be careful*?'

She picks at her wrist. 'Just … there are things that you … your father was a dedicated man – principled. He made mistakes but … just be careful who you trust that's all, before you make any promises.'

'You mean *him* – Greenhalgh?'

She looks hard at me, and I see her face is full of something like fear – for me or for her, I can't tell. 'If you want to know more about your dad, look online.' She leans in. 'Just be prepared for what you might find.' She smiles. There's lipstick on her teeth. 'Good luck.'

'Right.' We go on in silence and once we're out

of the lift, I ask her, 'Does the name *Red Gull* mean anything to you?'

She looks at me and shakes her head. 'Red Gull? No. Nothing.'

We walk back through the warren of corridors and stairs to the reception area. At the revolving doors, under the gaze of a security guard, she presses my hand briefly and squeaks off towards the lifts, and I'm left feeling like someone's just punched me in the head.

When I get off the train, I buy a packet of gum and walk the long way to Sophy's house. I ring the bell and wait. The door has that frosted glass in it so you can see who's coming and luckily it's her. She's standing on the threshold in a white dressing gown with her hair half tied up and half falling around her face and she looks amazing. She starts to say something but I never get to hear it because the way she's looking at me and standing so close, I make myself forget about everything else for just one second and do something so unlike me that it leaves me breathless. I bend and I stroke the hair from her face and I kiss her. On the mouth.

And you know what? She kisses me right back.

8

I'm stupid.

Why don't I ever just do the right thing? Why can't I *ever* stop thinking and worrying, and just *do* what my body wants me to do? I'm kissing a girl and I *know* she's got pretty much nothing on under her robe and the stairs are only a few feet away and every cell in my body is cheering me on … then why do I stop and apologise and start backing away and stuttering like a moron? Then she goes and asks me, am I OK and what's wrong? And it's making everything ten times worse.

I know why.

Because of my dad.

Because I can't get him out of my head and because of Annie Rivers and what she said, and the note and everything else that's got itself tangled up inside me like some toxic fur ball that I'm never going to be able to cough up.

She's looking at me now like she feels sorry for me

again. 'Ben, It's OK. I'm sorry. Let's just go and talk.
You're probably feeling –'

'Don't tell me what I'm feeling –' I say, and then,
'Sorry. Didn't mean it to come out like that. I just …'

I watch her face, so animated, and I know – if I didn't
know it before – she's way too good for me.

'Do you want to talk about it?' she says.

Christ.

I give a half smile and shake my head. 'It's OK. I'll
see you.'

That's it. She opens the door for me. Our hands
touch and it makes me want to pull her into a kiss
again but I stop myself before the whole sorry scene
repeats itself.

I'm on the path now, and she's standing on the
doorstep holding her robe at her neck and the wind
whips up her hair and brushes it across her face and I
go and say the lamest line in the book,

'I'll call you.'

Before I've turned round, she's closed the door. I
hear the glass clatter in its frame as I walk away.

When I get in I see Karen's left something in the
fridge for me, with a note saying did I want to go and
visit Dad's grave with them tomorrow.

I'm wondering if things can actually get much
worse. I've just screwed things up royal style with a
girl I like because of him, and now they want me to
go and stand in a cemetery and remind myself all over
again that he's dead.

I get my phone out and then I realise I don't even have her number. I could message her but Facebook's way too *up* for how I'm feeling right now.

I go into Dad's study, switch on the lights.

I think about them coming in here from Rees: wheezy guys with fat bellies and hairy arms loading all his things into boxes. And I decide I don't want to give them his stuff. Not one bit of it. Not ever. I open my laptop and send Greenhalgh an email:

> After I saw you, I thought about what you said and I'm not ready to part with any of my dad's stuff right now. Sorry. Ben Collins.

Dad worked at Rees for years. He worked for the army before that – that's where he did his degree. I don't know what he did the degree in exactly, something to do with science obviously, but he went on to do a PhD. That's what I know. That's all I know: the biography stuff, the CV, bits of it anyway. He didn't go out – didn't socialise. He found all that really hard – looking strangers in the eye, making small talk – like he couldn't see the point of it all. I remember Mum or Karen trying to talk to him about friends, gossip, whether it was going to rain on Saturday, how Mrs Blah had lost a stone … I'd watch him then, see his forehead furrowed, see him trying to make sense of it but I knew he was a hundred million miles away.

He never needed people on the outside but he needed us, and I let him down. It wasn't even anything major: it was just getting older I guess, thinking about girls, about friends, just wanting to hang out. I didn't want to talk to him any more about caterpillars or leafcutter ants and by then I'd had it with the blood tests and needles.

He never got it.

I was embarrassed I suppose, having a dad like that – I wanted to be with friends at *their* houses where their parents were normal.

Before he died, I just faded myself out. I made sure I wasn't in when he was about, stopped eating with him. Apart from the odd yes or no, I guess I must have gone six months without ever really speaking to him, quite an achievement when you think about it, in a three-bedroom house but I worked hard at it. And it drove him mad. So of course I kept doing it. I fucking *punished* the guy – just for being who he was, for being what he couldn't help.

Then one day he caught me smoking. Dad had a thing about smoking. No. Dad had a thing about *me* smoking. Because I was on the street when he saw me, by the end of it, every passer-by knew he had a thing about me smoking.

That was when I told him to stay out of my life and how I wished he was dead.

He said sorry then at once.

He stopped shouting, he put his hands on his ears and the counting started up, that soft whispered mantra of his.

He looked at me and I thought he was going to cry then but all he said was, 'I do love you Ben. I know I don't … I know I haven't …'

He never finished and I didn't say a word.

My thoughts are interrupted by a text which turns out to be from Sophy and when I see her name, I'm immediately, desperately, stupidly hopeful but when I open it, it's not what I want.

'WTF Ben?'

A rolling in my guts, needles in my skin. I write: *'Can I see you again? Want to explain',* then delete it and put: *'Sorry'* and send it.

'Sorry' is such a *non-word.* It means exactly nothing. It's just a thing you say when you can't say anything else. It's a stop-gap, shoulder shrug, amoeba of a word.

Of course she doesn't reply.

I go back to my laptop. Nothing new. I open Facebook and look at her page: pictures of her friends from her old school, all gurning at the camera. Her profile picture's a bad selfie – the camera's a bit close. It's blurred, like she turned or moved at the last minute. Red hair in a kind of halo and her lips parted but not smiling. I close it and go back to my own page.

My profile picture is the back of my head. Tells you all you need to know about where I'm at.

I'm about to close the laptop when I remember Annie Rivers: that sharp stare and what she said about looking online.

I try Red Gull first. There's a Red Gull Street in

San Francisco, there's a company in Finland that makes cosmetics, and Red Gull is the name of a boat that's sailing round the world for charity.

Then I put in my father's name: 'Dr David Collins'. There's a plastic surgeon in Utah who specialises in breast enlargement. The author of a book called 'Premier Football Grounds' is also David Collins and at the bottom of the first page, there's a blogging bird watcher. I go on to the next page and half way down I spot something: 'Mysterious Deaths of Scientists', and a list of names in dark blue font.

> There have been at least twelve deaths of people who worked for the Biotech arm of international pharmaceutical giant, Rees Global. There is speculation that they were all involved in top-secret bio-chemical research projects at the company. The death of the British defence journalist Aiden James, who was found hanged inside the wardrobe of his Chicago hotel room on April 1st, 2013 has also been the subject of speculation as being connected to the Rees deaths.

> After every death, police gave unofficial press briefings providing journalists with plausible, though unconfirmed, explanations for the accidents or apparent suicides. The major problem for police has been the lack of obvious signs of depression in most cases. Several British MPs demanded a government inquiry. Rees has issued a denial that these scientists had been involved in highly classified bio-tech projects and that the deaths were in any way connected, indeed they have denied the existence of any such projects at Rees Global or any of their subsidiaries.

Other theories have been posited that the deaths
were the work of European-based, extreme
environmental activists, although none such has
claimed responsibility.

A more outrageous theory suggests that a hostile
foreign power had developed an electromagnetic
'death ray' to drive the scientists to suicide. A
supermarket tabloid contends the ultrathin waves
emitted by the device interfere with a person's
brain waves, causing violent mood shifts, including
suicidal depression.

Are the scientists victims of corruption within a
highly secretive, highly competitive international
industry? Have they been brainwashed? Or are
the deaths nothing more than an extraordinary
coincidence?

His name is third on the list:

Dr David Collins: fifty-four years old. Associate
Research Director at Rees Global. Expert bio-
chemist. Death by carbon monoxide poisoning
on May 1st 2013, in his own garage, shortly after
returning from the US on a trip connected with his
work. Coroner's verdict: Suicide.

The list contains other names, other deaths, some
classified as 'Accidental', some as 'Open', and others,
like my father's, are 'Suicide'. I look down the list.

Gordon, Major John, forty-seven years old.
Seconded to the Research and Development arm
of Rees. Disappeared mysteriously in January

2012 while working on his doctoral thesis on
psychosurgery. Both mainland police and Interpol
launched searches for him in several countries,
without success. He eventually reappeared a month
later. He had been traced to a hotel in Moscow and
confirmed that he did not know precisely how he
had got there. He returned to his work and said he
would not discuss his disappearance or the death of
his colleague, Nora Blane. He died later in a high-
speed car crash after his brakes failed on March
17th of that year.

I look for Nora then. Nora jumped off Archway
Bridge in North London in December 2011. A small
puncture wound was reportedly found on her left
buttock but this was later dismissed as being from the
fall. Family and friends said that suicide was out of
character for her. She'd worked at Rees Biotech for
years and had just been promoted.

Was my father's death *mysterious?*

I know the Internet is full of crap conspiracy theories
but some of this feels pretty real.

The posting is by a Richard Bloomfield and it's titled
Keep Taking the Tablets. I plough on and eventually find
him on a message board full of loony conversations
about alien abductions and other weird stuff. I'm about
to leave it but then I think what the hell, and I write
him a line: *I want to talk about David Collins.*

That night I lie awake for ages trying to make sense
of what I've seen: Annie Rivers at Rees and what
she said about my dad, the list of names, the deaths.

And the Red Gull – is it connected? In spite of what Annie said about being careful, I want to know more.

When I finally get to sleep, I dream about him. About the day I found him. But in my dream the garage is changed. The old tumble dryer and the seedlings in pots are gone. It's empty – all steel and marble – except for the car and Dad at the wheel. But the garage doors are revolving ones and I can't get out of them. They send me spinning round, until I'm shouting and hammering on the thick glass to get out. My shouting wakes me up and I'm wrapped tightly in the duvet with my feet sticking out the end. My throat's dry and I'm sweating. The time on my phone says 3.15. I can hear Charlie snoring from his room.

And it comes to me there and then what I need to do.

The garage keys are on the hook in the kitchen and I grab them, feeling the lick of cold metal against my palm. There are two keys: the one for the main overhead door to get the car out and the one for the side door. I take a torch and go. I haven't set foot in the garage since that morning in May. None of us has.

I've never been as scared as I am right now and I don't even know why. My breath's coming in short bursts and in spite of the cold, I'm burning. I swing the torch.

Once I'm in there, I have to stop and stand in the silence and wait. The room leans into me. All around it, are things to do with him. It's full of him. His gardening tools are hung on hooks along the walls. Over my head is a false ceiling made from broad planks of wood on which are stuffed old bikes, a cot, a high chair. Things from the past, our past, tucked and folded away by him forever. The garage is made of breeze blocks and pitted concrete streaked with paint. The car's still there. There's just enough room to walk around it and get in on the driver's side. In front of the car, to my right, is a cobwebbed window with an old table underneath it. Dad's garden equipment is stacked to either side and the table is covered in paint pots and jars with nails and dowels and stuff. Under the table, is an old tarpaulin and, to the side, the tumble dryer. Holding the torch, I get on my hands and knees on the cracked concrete floor.

Apart from a stain of motor oil, there's nothing under the car. I run my hands along the shelves on the wall where coarse balls of dust like sheep's wool are clogged in corners. I turn round and slowly tug at the tarpaulin, trying not to make too much noise. It's lain under the table for as long as I can remember; it's enormous, covered in the husks of dead insects, and it crackles and scratches as I dislodge it. I pull it up with me and spread it out over the car bonnet.

Nothing.

Where it has been, there's a giant wet patch on the concrete. A woodlouse scuttles away from the light towards the dark of the tumble dryer. I get on my knees again, watch it go. And as it goes underneath the dryer, it swerves slightly like there's something blocking its way.

I reach into the damp dark under the feet of the dryer and feel a sharp scratch. It makes me draw back so suddenly that I hit my head on the table. I examine my hand. There's a faint line where whatever it is has nicked me: blood. I go back, feeling under the machine until I get it. I pull it out and let it roll on my opened palm.

A needle: antique, from his set.

Blackness. I'm back in his study. My arm's extended, blue and white. My father is squeezing the thin metal shaft into a vein and my blood is pulsing back into the patterned glass tube, his deft, careful hands, his tongue snapped between his teeth, and the breath between us coming and going.

There's a hairline crack along the glass from where it hit the ground.

What happened here?

What I thought I knew is blurring, rubbing itself out.

I go back into the house. In the hall is a low cupboard under the stairs where he kept the doctor's box. I squat down and tug the door open. With the torch, I scan the contents: a pile of used wrapping paper, a fake Christmas tree, old wellies. But the box is gone. I pull out the tree and the boots, squeeze myself half in and look. At the very back in the corner something winks in the light. I reach for it and my fingers close on something solid. It's a frosted blue glass bottle stopper, part of the set.

I lie awake for ages. And however much I twist and turn in bed, I can't get warm again. It's like that place sucked all the blood out of me. I try to think about Sophy: about her body and the way she pushed herself into me, the soft scratch of her robe, her waist, her breasts against my chest, her mouth ...

Just another thing I've messed up.

9

The weekend passes in a blur and on Monday I get to school at lunchtime and go straight onto the field. I see her in the distance talking to a boy called Darren I know from primary school. We were on speaking terms until Year Eight but if I go up to him now, I know he'll pretend he doesn't know who I am. He's going for that lean kind of Indie look but no one's told him you can have too many badges on your jacket.

I back away towards the fence, looking for someone – anyone – I know and I'm not ready when she comes over. 'Hi.' She's looking at me expectantly. I'm lost for words. She's so close to me and the closeness, her breath on my face, is electric. I can feel my pores open and the hairs on my arms prickle. She sees me watching her and I look away. I rub my face and stare at the ground.

'What is it?' she says, 'what's wrong? Listen, if you think … I mean *you came to me*, to my house.'

'I know. I know I did.' I flash her a look.

'*So?*' She waits.

'I … what did Darren want?' *I'm such a prick.*

'*What?* Fuck you. Just tell me, what was that about on Friday? Don't mess me about. Just be honest. If you don't want …'

I say, 'I do. I do want to see you … I want to be with you. I'm sorry. I'm really sorry. My head's just not right at the moment. Can we … could we try again?'

She stares at me and after a long pause says, 'I don't know. Maybe. Maybe …' and then, 'You know I could maybe help you, if you want.'

'What do you mean?'

'Well, that letter. If you wanted someone to … I don't know, *help?* Then I could do that.' I smile and she goes on, 'If it would help you get your head straight – *straighter?*'

I bring her in to me and she leans back, finds my eyes: 'OK?'

I nod. 'Yeah. Yeah. Good. OK.'

She extricates herself slowly and she's about to go but I call her back.

'What?' she says.

'There is something. Something else.'

So she comes with me. We leave school and I'm guessing by her nervousness this is probably the first time she's bunked school. We walk in silence to my house. I'm thinking about my room and wondering if I can ask her into mine the way she did with me. I decide against it.

'Is your brother –?' she says as I open the door.

'He's joining the Marines – leaving tomorrow.'

'Oh. Right. Then you'll be …'

'Yeah.'

'Cool,' she says too quickly.

'Yeah,' I say. Then, 'Is it?'

'Sorry. No. It's not cool at all. Sorry – stupid thing to say.'

We stand in the hall for about two years, while I fight the urge to carry her upstairs and remember to ask if she wants a drink. She sits at the kitchen table while I make a cup of tea.

'This house … your house: is it yours now? I mean …'

'Yes.' So don't want to talk about this. 'Yes and no. It will be. My aunt and uncle are sorting it. He didn't leave a will but –'

'None of my business,' she says quickly.

'No,' I say, gritting my teeth. 'It's OK. Fair question.'

She leaves it alone then. 'So, tell me what's happened then.'

I tell her about going to Rees and what I found out.

'He sounds super creepy,' she says.

'You think?'

'Yeah. And the deaths and everything. And they want to get in here and search the place? Don't let them – you're not *going* to let them?'

'No. I'm not. I told him.'

She smiles, and I fetch the needle I found. She turns it over in her hands. 'It's beautiful. And it belonged to your dad?' I nod. 'Did he ever use it?'

'Yeah. Sometimes.' I can't get it together right now to go into what he did do with it.

'So … but, maybe it's nothing. Maybe he dropped it?'

'Maybe. But look at this; I only noticed it this morning.'

I hold it up to the light for her to see. It's faint but there's a smear of a pinkish kind of sediment running along one side.

'It's just he was so careful about them, he cleaned them, sterilised them. It was part of a set.'

We look at each other. Sophy breathes, 'What do you think it is?'

'I don't know,' I say.

'OK. You're sure this is one of the set? I mean is there one missing?'

'The whole thing's missing. It's gone.'

'Oh.'

We look at the needle in silence for a moment. I take it, carefully pull and remove the plunger. Whatever it is has crystallised into micro-fragments along the length of the tube. I go to push my finger in when Sophy stops me.

'Ben, don't. Be careful. It could be poisonous. I – we – you could get it tested so, you know if there's like a deadly toxin …'

'Maybe,' I say slowly, replacing the plunger. 'Could be.' But I'm only half listening. Most of me is thinking about her.

I'm still thinking about her when she asks, 'Google it maybe?'

It's only then I remember Richard Bloomfield and the aliens and the message I wrote.

'Just got to …'

I get the laptop and we sit very close at the kitchen table as it flickers into life. I go to the site, feeling just a bit sheepish in front of Sophy, and click in. There's an answer waiting:

Who are you?

She looks at me. 'Go on,' she says.

I type: *My dad was David Collins. Can I talk to you about his death?*

None of this seems real. It's like some kind of video game you can pause then go out for chips and come back to later. He's logged as online, so we don't have long to wait for an answer:

Prove it.

I type: *I was the one that found him. I'm Ben James Collins.*

And? comes back.

I read what you wrote about deaths at Rees. I wanted to know what you know about it.

I send it and sit back. Sophy squeezes my shoulder and looks at me. I just stare at the screen until the reply comes up: *Can we meet? Are you being watched?*

There's a kind of nausea creeping up from the pit of my stomach into my throat. I type the word before I even know why: *No.*

Are you sure?

'Fuck this,' I say, then type, *Can I meet you or not*?

There's a long pause then the words: *I'll find you*.

And that's that. We wait but nothing else comes.

Sophy says, 'What did he mean, *watched*? This is scary.'

'Yeah. Maybe.'

'You think you can trust him?'

I rub my hands in my hair. 'Fuck knows.'

She comes even closer, links her fingers through mine. I turn to her and she says, 'I've got to go.'

'Yeah, sure. Sorry.'

'No,' she smiles, 'I've just got work to do. I'll call you.'

'I'll walk you.'

'I … thanks.'

I'm getting my keys when she says, 'You *should* get that needle tested.'

'Really?'

'Well, yeah, of course. It'll tell you what that stuff is – maybe it was used to …' She doesn't finish and I bristle.

'Kill my dad you mean?' I can't look at her. 'I don't know. Anyway … what's the point? Who am I going to tell? Supposing I *do* find out he was murdered by, whoever – the Mafia – whatever. Who's going to be interested and anyway, it's not going to …'

I stop, trying to slow my breathing.

'Not going to *what*?' she says.

'Change anything.'

She folds her arms. 'If you think that, then why are you even in touch with this guy? Why go to your dad's work? You *do* want to know; you're just scared of what you might find out.'

I shake my head and after a long time, I say, 'That's not it. Not really. I think I went into Rees because up until all this, I thought he … I thought he did it because of me – us – Mum; all that – but now I do think maybe it was something else. Maybe. And I guess, yeah, that made a difference. I just …'

'So. The needle's a part of that isn't it?'

'I guess. But where do you get it tested? A hospital? The police?'

She's holding the needle in her hand. I watch as it catches the light. 'What about,' she says slowly, 'what about the woman at your dad's work?'

'Annie Rivers?'

'Yeah.'

'She's a secretary.'

'She probably knows someone. She's bound to know more than we do anyway – and she was nice wasn't she?'

'I'll call her.'

'Don't say anything on the phone. Just say you want to meet her.'

I nod. There's a kind of blackness inside of me, rolling in like fog off the sea: a wariness, a watchfulness. It's not exactly fear, more like anticipation. Like I'm looking for a fight.

She picks up straightaway. I know her voice: 'Mr Greenhalgh's office?'

'Hey. It's Ben. Ben Collins. I was –'

Her voice is quick, choked. 'Hello Ben,' waiting, voices behind her fading. 'Yes?'

'I ... found something.' Sophy's fingers are spanned and tight on my arm. 'Something to do with my dad. Could I meet you?'

After a pause: 'Farnham Station tomorrow at six. Platform two.'

A buzz as she hangs up.

Later on, I'm going to bed and I'm half-way up the stairs on the landing when something makes me stop. There's a high window there which I can just see through. I stand to one side and look out across the road. And there, on the corner as the road curves away up the hill to where it ends in a wooded bank, is a car and someone in it – a hunched shape.

10

Charlie's leaving for Plymouth today and at eight in the morning, he's standing in my room. He hooks his kit bag up on his shoulder and looks at me. 'Taxi's here,' he says and he waits a minute. 'Right. Cheers then.'

I sit up in bed and try to smile. I don't feel anything. I can't feel anything. Then he goes and says what we both know he has to say, 'You going to be OK?'

I say, 'Yeah. Of course.' He looks away down the stairs and lowers his bag. He does a kind of fake yawn like he's bored and thinking about nothing in particular, and then he tries to catch my eye.

He says in a low voice, 'Listen mate,' he's waiting for me to say something – but that's not going to happen – then: 'You have to get over it you know, move on ...'

'Yeah, yeah, I know. I'm on it. I'm OK,' I say. But my guts are churning and my head's boiling. 'Good luck.'

'Cheers. I'll text you.'

I close my eyes and I can see little yellow sparks like chickens' feet: a mad mosaic of chickens' feet, dancing in a spotlight. I hear the taxi pull away and I roll out of bed and get dressed.

Sophy wanted to come with me and I said no and then yes, then no again. So she's come anyway.

Six o'clock and we're at the station. We stand at the top of the stairs to get a view of who's coming up. Ten past. Quarter past. A train screams in and we flatten ourselves against the wall as more people push up and down the stairs. Then I see her.

'Sorry I'm late,' she wheezes, looks at Sophy. 'Who's this?'

'Sophy, Annie Rivers,' I say. 'She's a friend.'

'I see, I see,' she says. A bearded man in a dark suit bumps past us and curses. She pulls us back into the corner, looks about her and asks, 'So, what is it?'

Suddenly it's like I'm looking down on us and the whole thing just seems so insane, it's all I can do not to laugh but she's looking at me expectantly.

Sophy prompts, 'Ben?'

I pull out the needle. 'This. I found it where he died.'

She takes it, bangles all knocking on her wrists, turns it over. Then she looks up at me sharply, says, 'Why me?'

I shrug. 'I don't know. You seemed ... you knew him.'

'There's something in it. See? It's been used,' Sophy says.

'Mmm. Interesting. Victorian, I think. Beautiful. Was it part of a collection?'

'Yeah, in a box. You seen this kind of thing before?'

'Once or twice – antique fairs, that sort of thing.'

'OK.'

'And you found it ...?' she says.

'Where he died. He was –'

She cuts in quick, 'I know. And the rest of it?'

Sophy says, 'Gone. Stolen. Missing anyway.'

'Ah. And this belonged to David? To your father?'

I nod.

'I see.'

We wait while she continues to turn the needle over in her veiny hands. Another train is shunting in and the smell of hot brakes fills the air. The platform empties again.

'When did you notice the box had gone missing?'

I look at Sophy. 'Yesterday.'

'And you'd not seen it since ...?'

'No.'

'So it could have been missing for a while?'

'I guess.'

'Mmm,' she says again.

'What do you think?' Sophy asks in a whisper.

She doesn't answer for the longest time, just stays staring at the needle, seemingly lost in thought, then she turns to me and says, 'I think it's all very odd. That's what I think.'

That blackness again.

'What happened when he died, Ben?'

I see his pale, bloodless eyes and his skin flat and

white behind the glass. Ten seconds. And then the loud thump of my heart and the slap of my trainers on the road as I ran. Out of there and away. Everything else was a blur. It was only much later, when I came home and everything was the same and different that I really understood, and that's how it'll be forever.

I look at her and shake my head. She leans in and pats my hand and it fucking chokes me – that's what pity can do for you.

'Are you sure this is what you want – to know more? You're prepared for whatever you might find?'

I nod slowly. She's brisk then and she holds up the needle. 'You want me to find out what's in it? It may be nothing but I'll see what I can do. I know someone.'

Sophy shoots a look at me and says to her, 'You think it might be poison? That pink stuff?'

A long silence and I'm chewing the inside of my mouth because I can't stand much more of this. Maybe Annie Rivers is right. Maybe I don't want this after all. Except ...

She fixes me with a stare. 'Supposing it is poison, Ben, what then? What will you do?'

It's like all the air is being sucked out of the sky. Like I'm 300 feet underground.

I say, 'Something.'

She straightens up. 'Leave it with me and I'll see if I can talk to someone – I'll be very discreet. Give me your number and I'll be in touch.' She puts the needle carefully into her bag and produces a scrap of paper and a pen.

I scribble down my number and she claws it into her fist and stuffs it in her bag. I look at her and her eyes narrow.

'Um ... I ...'

'Can you trust me? That what you're thinking?' she says quietly. 'Yes. You can trust me.'

'Not that. I just ... Do you think it's something to do with Rees, his death?'

'I don't know,' she says softly. 'I don't know. Like I said, you need to be careful. You ... *we* are dealing with things much bigger than –' and then she stops abruptly, she's looking at something behind me.

'What?' I say.

'Don't turn around,' she says. She grips my forearm, looks at me intently. '*Do* you trust me?' I nod, look at Sophy who's doing the same. 'Then go home. Stay away from Rees whatever you do. I'll be in touch when I can.' She walks quickly away.

But I do turn around. Just a second before our train pulls up, I see what she saw: across the tracks, at the far end of the opposite platform, in a long grey coat and holding a briefcase, is Evan Greenhalgh.

His head snaps to me and I see him pull out his phone.

There's nowhere to sit on the train so we hold on to the bars and I spend the time staring at the tops of people's heads. Every so often I glance at Sophy but she seems busy doing just the same thing. She doesn't look at me. And I know something's wrong. Walking home from the station, she turns to me and says, 'Shit, Ben.'

'What?'

Her blue eyes bore into me. 'This is serious, isn't it?'

I shrug like a kid, kick the pavement. 'I just ... Yeah, I guess.'

'Look, Ben,' her voice is softer now. 'Are you sure? About all of this? I mean, supposing you do find out he's been killed – that the needle had poison in it and you can somehow prove it, although ... of course, there isn't a body. Did they ... um ... cremate him?'

'Yeah. Yeah they did.'

She goes on, 'Suppose you *do* prove it's suspicious? What then? What happens then? Maybe she's right. Maybe you shouldn't get mixed up in this, Ben. *Ben*?' She puts her hand on my arm. 'I'm just not sure ... I'm not sure I want to be ...'

'It's OK,' I mumble. I don't blame her. I can't blame her.

But whatever happens I'm glad about the kiss. I'm glad that for once I just *did* something without coming up with twenty-five reasons why I shouldn't. I take her hand gently and squeeze it in mine.

I say again, only more audibly this time, 'It's OK,' and I surprise myself because I manage to smile. 'Look, I need to go. I'll see you later?'

And I walk away quickly and I don't look back.

As I walk and pavement gives way to grass and back again, I make myself think about Rees and what that note said about trust, and I'm suddenly not sure about Annie Rivers. Thinking about it now, leaving the only bit of evidence that my father's death might not have been suicide, with someone I only just met, seems incredibly stupid.

The house is empty when I get back.

11

I sleep badly again that night. I wake up sometime after four in the morning, in a coil of sheets, with my right arm dead from where I've been lying on it. As soon as my eyes are open, I'm sinking into watery nothingness: a cold, black bleakness that drags me under.

Sophy.

Sophy.

I push her out of my head and get out of bed for a pee. I go to the bathroom, massaging my arm to get the feeling back and I come out and stand there on the landing. There's a full moon and the night is still. I'm looking at nothing in particular and then, in the dark of the woods, where the road ends, I see a small flash of blue light.

I stare for ages after but there's nothing, just the woods and the quiet, like a locked box.

I fire up my Xbox and play for a while but I can't

concentrate. So I go down to the kitchen, make a sandwich and sit staring at a photo of my dad.

Next day I go to the Mall to see Maurice. I've not seen him for a while and I feel the need to check in with reality – or something like it.

'Here he is!' says Maurice to no one in particular, 'you all right?'

'Not bad.' It's the most I can manage.

'Come round the back. Let's have a sit down.' And there we are, like nothing's happened; it's all the same, it's always the same: biscuit crumbs, the old Pot Noodle still fermenting in the microwave, the magazines with familiar characters. Except Maurice. He seems a bit different. He's cleaner for a start. He smells different, like a kind of out-of-date air-freshener.

He fiddles with his phone then shoves it at me. 'There you go. That's my girlfriend. That. Is. My. Girlfriend.'

It's a picture of him and Jo smiling broadly. The wind's blowing their hair about and her arm is raised to push it back off her face. I think about Sophy again.

'Hastings.'

I look up. 'Eh?'

'Where we were. Went down on a day trip. She likes the junk shops. And I love a whelk. You can get the train down. Cheap day return. Tell you what mate, I'm doing that again.'

'Good.' I hand the phone back.

'How's things with you? Got exams have you?'

Maurice has a really hazy picture of what goes on at school. I can't imagine him ever going to school himself – it's like he's been this way forever. 'It's all about the exams these days. So I hear. Tea's up.' He hands me the tea, we load up with sugar and he gives me a chewed biro to stir it in. Just then someone calls him from the shop and he shuffles off, taking his tea. I sit back on the sofa and pick up a magazine. It's called *Star Gazing – UFO Monthly: The enthusiast's guide to alien sightings; abductions; UFO evidence; current research; conspiracy theories: Read Richard Bloomfield's report on the mysterious deaths of UFO investigators.*

I open it on the page. In the top left hand corner is a fuzzy picture: a big man with a huge jowly face and a biker moustache – he looks like a Redneck sheriff from somewhere in Mississippi. The article's written in purple with headings underlined and is subtitled: *Butch Worzinski's last stand.*

Butch lived in Nevada and was what they called a UFO/Human Mutilations Researcher. He'd been missing for weeks when a passing trucker found him hanging from a tall burnt-out tree in the middle of the desert. The really weird thing was that he was found hanging upside down, with sinister markings all over his body. The article's going into detail but Maurice comes back then and I put the magazine down.

Not before he sees what I'm reading.

'Ah. UFOs. Interesting isn't it? Got tickets for the biggie. Going to Leeds in the summer.' He waits like

I'm supposed to know what he's on about and when I make it clear I don't, he says, 'UFO event. Convention. Everyone who's anyone is going along. You'd like it.' He sits down and leans back contentedly and scratches at each elbow.

I point to the name on the article, Richard Bloomfield. 'Who's this guy?'

'Oh him. Dick Bloomfield – he's a nice chap. Super guy. American. Fluent in Klingon.'

I stay at Maurice's most of the afternoon and I find I've managed not to think about Sophy for at least thirty minutes at a stretch. After we've eaten our way through a ton of biscuits, I go home in the rain and when I get there I go upstairs to Charlie's room. His room is at the front of the house and it's the perfect place to watch the road. I haven't seen the car since last time but the more I think about it, the more I think the light I saw in the woods was a mobile phone. And yeah, of course it could be nothing but the way I'm feeling right now makes me think it *was* something: something to do with here. With me.

Sam comes over later, rams a pack of beer bottles on the table, and goes and wrings out his jacket on the carpet. 'S'up?' he says.

I shrug. 'Not much. You?'

'Come on dude. What about Sophy?'

I open a bottle. 'Nothing. Nothing happened.'

'Really?' he looks at me. 'Not what I heard.'

'What's that then?'

'That you punched Ed Kramer cos he wouldn't let you sit with her, and then you were seen heading out of school together.'

I knock back a slug of beer, feel the cold of it washing my insides. 'Not how it sounds.'

'She blow you out?'

'Fuck, Sam. Give it a rest.'

'All right, all right. Just asking. Thought she was in to you. Seemed that way.' I fold my arms and wait. He says quickly, 'My dad got me *Halo*.'

'Yeah?'

We play on the Xbox till late. Dawn's breaking when he goes and I finally fall asleep.

It's three in the afternoon when I'm woken by a faint but persistent noise. I lie there and listen and it stops, and then I think I hear something downstairs, something falling, then – sharp now – a kind of scraping.

For a moment I'm paralysed. I think about curling up and pulling the duvet over my head and waiting till whatever or whoever it is goes away. Then curiosity and fear get the better of me. Very quietly, I roll out of bed, grab a T-shirt from a pile on the floor and slip it on, open my door a fraction and listen.

There's someone in the study.

I creep down the stairs holding my weight on the banisters. The door to the study is closed. I wait, feeling the blood ticking up and down my neck, while I figure out what I'm going to do. I need a weapon of some sort. There's an umbrella stand in the corner by the front door and in it, there's a heavy walking stick my Gran used to use. I pull it up as quietly as I can but it rattles against the sides as it comes out, and the noises stop suddenly.

I hear footsteps walking towards the study door.

I wait. I think I can hear breathing from the other side. I'm holding the stick so tightly my skin's bleeding sweat into the grain. Then a sudden clatter from inside makes me jump and it jolts me enough to get me charging through the door waving the stick.

The room's empty. The window's open and a hundred yards away in the distance, there's a figure in black sprinting up the hill to the wooded bank beyond. I watch him go, fixed to the floor, the stick still in my hand.

I back up to the threshold and look around the study. There are dark grooves in the floor where it looks like someone's tried to lever up the floorboards. There are papers spilling from the desk, reaching out from every drawer and shelf, the pictures are crooked and a glass specimen case is shattered.

What was he looking for and did he find it? I'm thinking *not*, if he was still at it when I disturbed him.

So.

There has to be something here to find.

For the rest of the afternoon and into the evening, with the doors and windows locked, and an extra-large bag of assorted crisps for company, I sit on the floor and go through his papers carefully. The first few I come to are about house stuff: MOT for the car, bills, certificates, insurance. I put them to one side while I scour another pile: more routine stuff.

Then I go through everything else, scanning each piece of paper for something – *anything* – I have no idea what. Every so often, I come across his workings: chemical formulae scratched out in lines that cross and cover the paper like little rows of teeth.

At the end of it all, I've found nothing that looks so important that anyone would go to all that trouble for. But what do I know?

I make myself beans on toast, stand in the kitchen, eating them folded into a sandwich, and thinking. As I lean into the sink to catch the stray beans, I see myself reflected in the dark glass of the kitchen window: pale face and hunched shoulders. I stand up straight and push my hair off my forehead. My eyes are ringed with dark shadows and my cheeks are hollow. I've lost weight. *Is this it?* I'm seventeen and I look like Keith Richards.

I take out my phone and stare at it. There's a silence in the house like all the noise in the world's been sucked out of it. Like how I feel: dry, drifting, cut loose. Except when I kissed Sophy. Just for a moment I thought I saw a kind of way out of it or through it. Like when you're on the train and you're deep in a tunnel and there's nothing but blackness outside, then just for an instant, you see a light and a spark fly up from the tracks, and there's the moss on the bricks on the tunnel wall, and you sort of know where you are again. Like you can *find* yourself. It's like I saw the thread – the way back.

I send her a text: *Are you free tonight?*

I leave the phone on the counter and I do forty circuits of the kitchen (I'm counting) and I'm on the forty-first, when it buzzes. I make myself walk to it slowly:

Can't tonight. Going out. Maybe tomorrow?

Going out? Going out with *who?* The quietness pushes on my chest and I have to go outside and breathe.

There are no stars. Just a blue blackness.

I go back in, close the kitchen door and go upstairs.

I'm playing a game when Charlie comes into my head. He's the most normal person I know. Nothing ever seems to back up on him. I think about the last thing he said to me and I send him a text: *Hey. How's it going?*

It's just a flare going up in the dark because I know he won't have his phone but I send it all the same, then carry on with the game.

Of course there's no reply.

But that doesn't stop me waiting for one.

It's much later when another text comes through.

A number I don't recognise: *Are you at home?*

I text back: *Who is this?*

Richard Bloomfield

Shit.

Where are you?

Outside.

12

For a moment I wonder what it means. And then I realise he means *outside*. Just then, I hear a sharp rap on the front door. I go downstairs, hesitate a moment, then open it. A large, flabby man is standing on the doorstep. The moustache is gone, he's wearing a baseball cap, a grubby anorak, and his belly hangs way out over his belt. He's carrying a charity shop tote bag.

As soon as I open the door, he pushes in past me and closes it behind him. We stand awkwardly, staring at each other in the narrow hall.

He pulls off his cap and sticks out his hand. 'Richard Bloomfield. Call me Dick.'

I suppress an urge to laugh and I fold my arms across my chest.

'OK, OK,' he says. 'You're wondering how I got your number. Because I know how to do that shit. Ten years in the CIA. Where can we talk?'

Before I can say anything, he's pulled something

out of his bag that looks like a calculator and he's waving it around his head. He walks in and out of the sitting room, the kitchen, then into the study, draws the curtains and switches off the light so the room is lit by the light in the hall. He runs the thing over the skirting board and it sets up an intermittent beeping.

'Uh oh.' A pause. 'Here we go.'

He moves the mess of papers to one side and kneels down by the plug socket, partly exposing two fleshy buttocks covered in wiry ginger hair. He fishes a screwdriver out of his pocket, unscrews the socket and after a while stands up, hitching his trousers. It looks like an ordinary socket to me but he's holding it like it's a human kidney.

'*What*?' I say.

'You may well ask. This is a GSM infinity transmitter.'

'A *what*?'

'A GSM transmitter. It fits into a standard UK 240 volt mains transmitter. You can call into this unit from anywhere in the world and listen to what's being said in the room. Looks good, huh?'

I shrug. It still looks like a socket. He runs the calculator thing over it and it squeaks again. 'Place is a mess,' he says.

'Yeah. Yeah I know. Had a break in.'

He nods and scratches his belly. His small eyes flick up and down on me. 'Ben, somebody's interested in this house, in your dad. What's the story? What do you know?'

'I don't know anything. I literally have no idea. But what you said in your blog – about brainwashing, foreign powers …'

'Bullshit. Baloney.'

'Eh?'

'Eco-terrorists? Death rays? All that? Come on, Ben. I had to put that in. There's no one else involved in this.'

He sits down on the desk chair, puts his hands on his stomach and pushes back. 'You know what Rees do, right?' he says.

'They're a pharmaceutical company.'

'Well. Yes, they are. They are,' he says, and waits a minute before going on like he's giving a lecture or something. I stare at him and he says, 'Let me tell you what I know. Rees is a very large organisation. Big pharmaceutical wing – all kosher. All above board. But it's the Biotech arm that's the interesting part. It's got its fingers in lots of pies. Some of them perfectly legit. But they have other … branches that are a little shadier. They got involved in the late nineties in some minor projects to do with bio-chemical warfare but we don't think it stopped there. They're very coy about it for obvious reasons but people like me – the little people – are interested in it, we think they've made billions from it. Ever read about the Lebeque incident?'

I swallow. 'No.'

'OK. Not surprising. Not many people have. Lebeque is a small village in France in the Massif Central. It's set in a deep valley, fairly isolated. Very beautiful.

I've been there. A few years ago now, nearly 300
inhabitants caught a cold. Six weeks later, ninety were
dead. Men, women, children, young and old. And you
know what else? The local paper reported sightings of
a strange, pinkish coloured cloud overhead. People's
breathing was affected. Noses and eyes running, sore
throats, vomiting. No explanation.'

'What are you saying?'

'Just that ...' he starts. I can't see straight. It's like the
veins in my eyes are swelling up. 'Ben?'

'My dad, is it? Is that my dad you're talking about
now?'

'Well ...' softly, 'but, Ben, you wanted to know.
You ...'

'I wanted to –' I start, and I'm angry and all I want
is to shut the guy down but then, then I remember:
'I did see something, I found something – hidden in
his desk – a newspaper cutting about a mystery illness
in France.'

'He kept it? Mmm. Yes, that would be it, although
illness is a slight misnomer here.'

'And you think –?'

'Well, we think it was down to Rees. To ...'

He doesn't finish but I know what he was going to
say. I swallow it though. 'OK. So, if ... why aren't the
police involved? Why don't they do something?'

'Fair question. The police wouldn't stand a chance.
Rees is airtight. All this – what I write about – it's easily
dismissed as a conspiracy theory. They looked into it

of course but they didn't find anything. You want to get into this – you want the truth – you've got to trust me and go with it. There are ways. We think they were testing something in Lebeque, you see: one of their little recipes. And it went wrong, oh boy, did it go wrong. It was all hushed up at the time – like I say, they're pretty untouchable. But by then we think they were working on developing really out-there intensive germ warfare. Anthrax, for example, has spores which are perfect for dispersal by aerosol; and then there's tuberculosis, cholera, yellow fever – you name it.'

I swallow and wait. He starts slowly. 'So. Your dad. I think – *we think* – he might have been part of a team involved in cutting-edge research about the methods of spreading these diseases and developing new ones: aerosols, bombs – big business. This isn't just about soldiers shooting at each other, it's about destroying families, whole communities, cultures. Your dad was a clever man. I didn't know the guy but I think maybe, like others, he'd sold his soul and he knew it. It's my guess he was working on something big when he died.'

I'm shaking my head violently by the end. 'No. I don't think so. I don't … it can't be. You've got the wrong guy, mate. He wouldn't – he was … he was working on cancer treatment. They told me at Rees.'

'You *went* there?'

'They … came here. They asked me to go and see them.'

'Ben, you don't look stupid but that was a stupid thing you did there.'

I feel cold. 'Don't tell me what I can or can't do.'

'OK, man.'

I don't hear myself shouting till I'm done. 'Don't patronise me either. You've got no proof. My dad was ... my mum died of cancer. He was all about finding a cure. He was ...'

He looks at me with sad eyes. 'Sure. Maybe. But ...' and he leaves it there, and I buckle. My eyes are closed and I'm outside the room, outside the house, getting further and further away and I can still hear him saying what he's saying but it's like I'm not a part of it, like it's nothing to do with me, like the person he's talking about, the person who did those things, is nothing to do with me.

And then I'm back there in the room facing him. He's stopped talking and he's waiting for my reaction. There's a pain starting behind my eyes that crackles and fizzes in my brain. I have to lean against the wall to steady myself.

I leave Dick in the study while I go to the kitchen and I dip my head into the sink and turn on the cold tap. I stay there for ages, feeling the cold liquid flow over me, tickling my neck and reaching under my collar and down my back. The pain subsides and I turn off the tap but I stay with my head bent over the sink watching the water slide from my hair. I'm suddenly aware of him in the room behind me.

'Shock, huh?'

I rub my hair and turn to face him.

He says, 'You know your dad's not the only one who died like that?'

'I know.'

'But you're the only one brave enough or curious enough to ask some questions. People are scared.' He pauses and stretches. 'Look, maybe I'm wrong about him, maybe I'm way off but you want to know what really happened that day, don't you? If nothing else?'

I'm reminded of what Annie Rivers said. She knew. They all knew.

'So you know – we both know – a lot of other people went the same way, Ben. Rees ruined a lot of lives. I know it's a shock, I know you don't want this. But these are bad people, and this is just the beginning. You could *use* this – you could nail Rees for good. *We could nail them.* Ben?'

I look away to the window. And there's my reflection again. It's *his* face staring back at me. Can I separate the man from what he did? Can I separate me from what he did? Can I live with this? Can I carry this around with me for the rest of my life?

And yeah. If it's all true, then I do want to nail Rees.

I turn around and Dick's gone. I can hear him in the study. I take a deep breath and go back into the room. He's leaning over Dad's desk, fiddling with papers with one hand and scratching his arse with the other. He doesn't look at me when I come in.

'You OK?'

I steady myself. 'Yeah, I think so.'

'We going to do this?'

In answer, I go to help him with the papers. He's pulled out the ones covered in equations and is studying them carefully, his eyebrows going up and down.

'You say you went through these? You didn't find anything?'

I'm about to say no, when I remember the note. 'Hold on.' I run upstairs and grab it off my table, show him. He unfolds it carefully.

'Someone shoved it through the letter box,' I say.

He nods, humming to himself. 'Red Gull? *Find the Red Gull*? What is that?'

'No idea.'

'Trust no one – they were right about that,' he says. 'You've never heard this before, Red Gull?'

'Never,' I say.

'Hmm. Might be nothing but it looks like maybe it's a password. Did he have a laptop?'

'He had one – a Sony – but it's not here any more. I don't know where it is.'

'Stolen?'

'Maybe.'

'Yes? When? Today? Your break-in?'

I shake my head. 'No. I haven't seen it since before he died.'

'You remember who was there that day? Who came? The cops?'

The truth is – the real truth of it is, I have no idea, because when I saw him, I ran. I didn't call the ambulance or the police. I shouted for Charlie, then I ran.

I shake my head. 'I don't … I don't …'

'OK, OK,' he says, 'but they're coming back for more. They want something. He must have kept something back, hidden something. Was there anything else?'

'There was something.'

'Oh yeah?'

'I found a syringe. In the garage.'

'When he died?'

And then I have to tell him the whole thing, about the medical box, about the syringe and what was in it and what my father did with it – the blood tests and the injections when my mum was sick. He shakes his head when I tell him about Annie Rivers.

'Sleeping with the enemy,' he says. I look up but he waves a fat hand. 'You mind if I take another look around?'

He's already been looking without my permission, so I guess he doesn't really need it. I leave him to it and go back to the kitchen. I avoid looking in the window this time but I can see Dad everywhere. He's in the crack in the wall over the cupboard; his eyes are in the jars over the sink. I'm putting on the kettle when I hear my phone. I look at the clock. It's a quarter to ten.

It's a text from Sophy: *Are you at home?*

I look at it, delete it, put the phone on the counter and go about making myself and Dick a cup of tea.

I need to think. Apart from anything else, I'm angry with her for being out with someone else and I want her to know it. I know she's not my girlfriend. And while nothing she's done really gives me the right to be angry, it feels good for a bit, kind of powerful.

There's a strange, soft, whooping sound from the other room and Dick calls me in. He's standing with his back to me.

'Take a look at this.' I lean over his shoulder and see where he's pointing. In his hand is the tiny drawer from the hidden compartment and underneath it, is a thick rectangular wafer of wood. 'You got a penknife, tweezers or something?'

I go back to the kitchen and find a vegetable knife, ignoring the chime from my phone to say I've had a second text. Back in the room, I watch as he prises the splinter out. It's a carefully cut piece of wood that fits snugly into its hole. It's paler than the rest of the wood but you'd still have to look hard to see it. In the shallow cavity it covered, is a small black object, no thicker than an After Eight Mint. He picks at it with the knife until it drops into his palm: an SD card.

He looks at me and grins. 'Bingo.'

At that moment, my phone rings. It's Sophy. I go back and get it, answer it. All I can hear is a kind of muffled breathing that sounds like someone running.

Then, 'Ben! Ben! Please, someone's after me. Ben?'

Then the phone goes dead. I go quickly to the last text: *I need you. Please answer. S*

13

I ring back at once but it goes to voicemail. I try again and again and again.

'What's going on?' Dick says.

'A friend. I think she's in some sort of trouble.'

He frowns. I try one more time and she answers in a whisper, 'Ben?'

I can feel the muscles knotting inside me. 'Where are you? What's up?'

She's crying, I can hardly hear her. 'I'm in Cloak Hill – the cemetery.'

'What are you doing there?'

'Just ... can you come and get me? Please?'

'Of course, just –'

'I called the police but ... can you ...?'

'Sophy it's OK. Don't move. I'm coming.'

I say to Dick, 'Have you got a car?'

He nods, he's been listening. 'I know it. Let's go.'

I follow him as he half runs, half waddles across the

drive. It's starting to rain. Up the hill, a car is waiting: a large, four-wheel drive with bull bars front and back. He heaves himself into the driver's seat, pulling his bulk up by the steering wheel. I get in and before I've closed the door, he's reversing down the hill at forty miles an hour. With the bitter smell of burning rubber in our nostrils and Fleetwood Mac on the stereo, we're out onto the main road in the dark.

We're about half way there, when he says, 'Taking too long.'

Without slowing down, he turns down a side street which ends in a barred gate onto the heathland beyond. He doesn't hesitate but drives straight at the gate and crashes through onto a scrubby wasteland with pine trees and stubby gorse bushes.

He drives across the heath and off onto a slip road leading to the motorway, and swings the car out into the fast lane. The wind screams and steam smokes in plumes from the bonnet.

He looks across at me. 'You all right?' I nod. He says, 'Cool. We're almost there. Try her phone.'

I try it twice but it goes to voicemail. He shifts in his seat, says, 'This something to do with you, you think?'

'I don't know. I hope not.' I'm so strung out I can't think straight.

He turns off the motorway and as we draw up to the roundabout at the top of the filter lane, there's a car waiting at the lights up ahead of us.

'Hold on to your hat,' he says grimly, guns it into

fifth gear, steers around the waiting car and shoots off, skimming the roundabout, with me hanging onto the seat.

We pass the dark huts of Aldershot Barracks at 12.15 on the car clock, and before long the sign for Cloak Hill comes up.

My text goes. *I'm near the mermaid. Hurry.*

The gates of the cemetery are padlocked. We get out and go in through a side door on foot.

Cloak Hill Cemetery is old. It's built on a stretch of sloping ground that runs down to a railway line. In among the graves, there are tall, twisted trees with branches that curl and claw skywards.

With the rain coming down in sheets on my face and my back, and with Dick behind me, I run like a madman along wet paths. White gravestones loom out of the ground at odd angles like broken teeth and I can see any amount of stone angels and crosses but no mermaids. Suddenly, up ahead, to my right, a dark figure runs across the path and disappears behind the graves that fall away into the trees. There's something in his hand.

I leave Dick behind to get his breath back and I set off in pursuit, leaving the path and weaving through the gravestones. I stop for a moment and listen. It's so quiet here I can hear the soft snapping of the electricity cables on the railway line below. I crouch down and wait. There are fewer headstones here, and from where I am, I can see the train tracks through the trees.

A loud clap rings out in the silence. And then, quite close, a sound like the panting of an animal. I tuck myself in behind a stone and look out.

I see the figure again: a man, not much older than me, running in my direction. His face is white in the moonlight and I see now he's carrying a gun.

He hasn't seen me and he turns at some noise behind him. He raises his arm and I jump him. He's smaller than me and surprised, and I manage to push him over. The gun flies out of his hand and lands a short way away in a patch of brambles. He's up on his feet at once, looking for it but I'm ready and I punch him hard in the face and he reels back but regains his balance and takes off into the gloom.

It's then that I hear a crackling in the undergrowth to my left. I go forward slowly, keeping low until I see it: a clumsy carving of a mermaid over the ruin of a stone arch. The arch is covered in weeds that wind up and around it from the ground. I go through and I almost miss her.

'Ben!'

Slowly, she stands up. Her face is bloodless and there are leaves in her hair and her jacket's torn at the sleeve.

'Fuck,' I say. 'Did he hurt you?'

I hold her and she's shivering. I wrap my hoodie around her and wait. In between breaths she tells me what happened.

'I had this text. I didn't know the number but it was a guy I used to know from years ago, an old friend.

He said could we meet up. He said to meet him in the Kings Head on Cloak Hill and we could go for a drink.'

'Then what happened?'

'I got there. I waited and waited and he didn't turn up. I was going to go home. I mean he wasn't a … he was just a nice guy, I mean, it wasn't like –'

'Go on.'

'I started walking back to the bus stop when a car stopped and a man asked if I wanted a lift into town. I said no but he went on at me – wouldn't leave it. He said the buses weren't running – just stuff like that. I didn't like it, I just ran. There was another man in the car and he got out and chased me. I came in here. I'd been here before so I remembered the mermaid. Ben, I don't get it. What do these guys want?'

'I don't know. I don't know. Sophy, if this has anything to do with me … I'm really sorry. Beyond sorry.'

'I'm sorry too. The other day – at the station – when I said that, I was just scared. I *am* scared.'

'I promise I won't let anyone hurt you Sophy.'

I'm holding her so close I hear her heart beating, and she lifts her head then and I bend to kiss her but as our lips meet, I hear a noise behind me.

'There you are,' says Dick. 'You had me spooked. You hear the gunshot? Jeez!'

He looks at the two of us. I say, 'Dick, Sophy, Sophy, Dick.'

He sticks out his hand and she takes it but she doesn't let go of me.

'How you doing?' he says.

'I'm OK. Thanks for … you know. Thank you.'

I tell him what Sophy's told me.

'Mmm. Doesn't sound good.'

'You think it's –?' I say.

'They're desperate. They think you know something and that she's a way to get to you. For what it's worth, I don't think … the gun … it would have just been to scare you. You understand?'

Sophy says, 'It worked.'

He pads off a little way, then paces back. 'We need to get you two to a safe place somewhere,' he says. 'We all need some time to think. I've got somewhere.'

'What do you mean?' I say.

'If this is what I think it is,' he says slowly, 'they're serious. They're watching you, they've been in your house, they were about to use your girl to get to you. You've really got no idea what they might want? Are you *sure*?'

I nod. 'Yeah. I mean, no. I don't know.'

'It's not safe right now for you two to be at home. They're not going to stop looking for you.'

'Don't be daft,' I say. 'Just take us back.'

'All I'm saying is, just let me get you away for a while – away from where they'll be looking for you.' He looks at me hard. 'I'm not kidnapping you. You'll be safe. I'm on your team, Ben. Just trust me, OK?'

I look at Sophy and back at Dick. 'This is insane.'

He folds his arms. 'What do you think?' he says

to Sophy, and she goes and says, 'I'll need to phone my Mum.'

He raises an eyebrow at me, then starts to walk back to the gate. He calls to me over his shoulder, 'You coming?'

'Sophy?' I say. She's standing between him and me. I lower my voice. 'Do you really want to do this? I mean ... he's ... I don't even properly know the guy. He might be –'

She shrugs. 'He's helping you isn't he?'

'Yeah, but ... *Trust no one* – that note. I mean, what if –?'

'You don't even know who wrote it. Listen, this – what just happened – was really scary, and I'm soaking, and my mum and dad are out and I don't want to go back to an empty house and ...'

'OK, OK,' I say. 'We're going.'

We go back through driving rain and out through the side gate to the car. I get in the back with Sophy, and Dick starts the engine. We pass a police car coming the other way and I look at Sophy. Her face is paper-white.

She phones her mum to say she's staying at a friend's for a couple of nights and I put my arm around her when she makes the call.

I lean forward to Dick. 'Where are we going?'

'It's a little way away – hour or so.'

Amazingly, I fall asleep, and I wake up with a crick in my neck and the smell of Sophy's hair on my clothes. She's asleep, crooked against the window with my hoodie as a pillow and her feet up on the seat and up front, Dick's humming to himself. We've left the main road and we're driving across a ploughed field. It's still raining and the car's bucking and jolting over the uneven ground, throwing up a muddy spray onto the windscreen. He turns a corner and pulls up beside what looks like a kind of barn. I climb out, leaving Sophy just waking, and stand next to Dick. From what I can make out, it's a ruin: no more than a brick shed, open on one side and smelling of engine oil and straw. Inside, filling the space, is the rusting bulk of an old combine harvester, its giant spines bent and broken.

High above, along a row of dark trees, I hear an owl calling. I look at Dick. I guess when he said we needed a safe place, I imagined at least a bed. With the combine, there's barely room to stand up, let alone lie and sleep. Sophy gets out and stands next to us, rubbing her arms.

'God it's freezing,' she says. 'I need a wee. Where are we?'

'Follow me,' he says.

14

As Dick strides into the barn, Sophy grabs my arm, pulls me back and whispers, 'God, were we mad? What do you think?'

Well. Let me see, I think he's going to take us inside and torture us with farming implements, kill us, burn our bodies and plough us into the ground. I don't say that. Of course.

I say, 'It'll be fine. It's fine.' Great. Really comforting. She frowns but follows me in. Dick is nowhere to be seen.

It's a small space and as far as I can see, there are no other doors leading off it. I peer into the gloom but there's no one there. We look at each other, puzzled, and then I hear him.

'Come on, you guys.' The voice is coming from below us, from underground.

'Come on,' he calls again.

'Here! It's here!' cries Sophy, pointing to a thin bar

of light on the ground. It gets wider as a wooden trap door is pushed up towards us and a meaty freckled forearm is exposed. Inside, there's a set of stairs that spiral down into a kind of wood-lined cabin. Dick stands back to let us go down.

It's lit by gas lamps, and there's a bed, a small couch, a stove and a sink. There's a picture on the wall – a family photograph – a Mum and Dad and three young sons, all wearing matching ski jumpers, all grinning and all fat. I think I spot Dick in the centre of the group. His two front teeth are missing. No one who has that on his wall is going to be an axe murderer.

Sophy's the first to speak. 'This is great.'

'I set it up a few years ago. I've got friends who need to hide out from time to time. You'll be perfectly safe.'

'Is there a loo?' Sophy asks.

'Through there,' he says.

When Sophy leaves, we stare at each other.

He says, 'OK. Here's the thing: I need to speak to some contacts of mine. I want to know more about what Rees are after and just what exactly they're trying to hide. I've got the memory card and I'm going to go back and try and get a look at it. Can I leave you both here? I may be gone a while.'

'Well … I don't know. How long?' I say.

'I don't know. Maybe twenty-four, maybe forty-eight hours. There's plenty of food and the stove works pretty good. Just stay out of sight. You understand me?' Sophy comes back then and he tells her what he's told me.

We stand and listen to him drive away, and then there's nothing. The gas lamps flicker and throw weird shapes on the walls. I have that feeling again, like I'm in some kind of film or video game. Like someone's pressed pause, left me here and gone home for their tea, and when they come back, I'll be propelled off into another scene.

I sit down on the bed and look at the floor. There's a kind of hand-made rug with a picture of the sun with a face on it. Then Sophy's feet are on the rug in front of me. More than anything, I want to touch her, be close to her but she says, 'Do you want some tea?'

A cup of tea is pretty much the last thing I want right now but I look up, nod my head. She busies herself with the tea things and the quiet between us is poison.

Cups and spoons and my heart banging in my chest.

She hands me a cup and smiles at me like I've been in a train crash or something, then sits down on the couch facing me. The quiet still hums on around us. And the space between us seems to get wider and wider, until she says, 'He's weird, isn't he?'

'Dick? Yeah. Yeah.' I manage a sort of laugh-snort.

'I'm sure it'll be ...' She breaks off, and I nod vigorously and look at my tea. Then out of nowhere she says, 'You must miss him – your dad?' I look at her and I'm blinking hard. 'What was he like?' she says.

'He was ... you'd probably think he was odd.'

'Odd?'

'He was … it's hard to explain. He was really clever but he didn't get people, you know? If they were upset or bothered or just being sarcastic, he didn't … I don't know … it's like he just didn't understand – bit *autistic* I suppose.'

'You were close though?'

I can see him then. Years ago. Mum's there and it's a school parents' evening. I'm talking to a couple of friends and she's chatting to their parents but he's standing apart, straight backed, tapping his fingers against his sides with this fixed grin on his face, and I catch his eye and he looks so fucking sad and out of place.

'Yeah. Yeah. I think so. Yeah. We were.'

There's silence and to do something I slurp up some tea, and the hot liquid nearly chokes me, and just when I think I might try to get closer to her, she says, 'So, what are you doing next year?'

It's the '*So*'. Like she's some kind of careers counsellor. And next year? I can't even think about next *week*. The whole idea is beyond depressing, not least because I guess Sophy, along with everyone else, will be going to University or on a *gap year*. And since I'll either be leaving school with no A levels and a really bad attendance record or, depending on how all this pans out, I'll be dead, there isn't really a lot to talk about.

'I don't know,' I say.

Quiet again. She blows on her tea and it comes out like a whistle. Her hair's wet against her neck and I think about my fingers gently pulling it back, and kissing her.

'You must have some idea?'

I shake my head. 'Not really.' I pull myself together and ask her. 'You?'

'Mmm, well, Mum and Dad want me to go to uni but I want to see the world a bit before I do that. I mean, I just think we're on this earth to have ... experiences, you know, do stuff. I want to keep bees, I want to go to America, I want to start a band, I want to learn Japanese, I want to deliver a baby ... I –'

And then she stops because, before I even know it, in spite of myself, I'm laughing. I'm actually crying and laughing at the same time because being with her, being next to her makes me feel brave and excited about life for once. She's brilliant. And I tell her.

'I just see the good side I suppose.' I guess that means she thinks I see the bad side, which is probably true. But maybe that won't always be the way.

I rub my head and say, 'I like Art.'

'Really?'

'Yeah, I like painting and drawing.'

And then she kind of ruins it. 'That's great. So, what about going to art school?'

Art school. Yeah. That's the solution to everything. Fill in a fucking application form. Great. But I don't say that. I just smile and say, 'Yeah. Maybe'

A long silence. She says, 'Ben, I'm sorry,'

'About what?'

'I just realised I sounded like I was trying to organise you. I'm really not. I just ... I like you. I guess I just want you to be happy and I – sorry.'

I look at her, straight at her. 'I like you too. You kind of saved my life, I think.'

She puts her tea cup down and it clunks against the spoon, and she comes over to me, kneels down and takes my face in her hands and kisses me, really kisses me. I kiss her back and hold her close and my face is in her hair and she smells so good.

For what seems like a long time, we're very still, me sitting and her kneeling and leaning into me with her head on my chest. Then I can't help myself and I kiss her again. She gets up, turns away, and just when I think I've done something wrong, she starts to undo the buttons on her top.

'I can't …' She's fiddling with the little buttons on her cardigan. I get up and face her. Slowly, before I really know what I'm doing, I pull her into me. She's shivering now and I slip the buttons free. We look at each other.

Under her cardigan she's wearing a T-shirt and she puts up her arms like a child and lets me pull it off over her head. Her hair stands up with the static like a fiery halo and I run my hand over it to smooth it down. The skin on her back feels so soft and the tiny hairs on her arms push up at my touch and I feel her warm breath on my skin.

'Ben, I –'

But something stops her. And then I hear it. It's faint but there's no mistaking it. A car. Coming this way.

15

'Shit.'

'Could be a coincidence?' she says, but she knows the answer to that as well as I do. We're on an abandoned farm in the middle of the night. The track doesn't even go anywhere.

She tries again. 'Dick? Coming back?'

I shake my head. 'Different engine. Come on.'

She struggles into her T-shirt and for a split second as I watch her, the wanting her and the aching, drowning disappointment at what could have been, almost ends me right there but the car is louder now and I reckon we've got seconds. I kill the lights and there's nothing, just our breathing and the smell of damp earth.

We climb back up the ladder. I go first and I'm not ready for what I see. There's not one but two sets of headlights coming towards the barn. I turn and pull Sophy up and, keeping low, we run past the side of the combine, round the back of the building and into a line of trees just as the cars come to a stop.

We crouch in a ditch, our feet in stinking water, and watch. Four men with flashlights get out, talking in low voices. One crosses over to where we were, squats down and beckons to the others.

'They knew we were there. Do you think Dick –?' Sophy whispers. I'm still holding her hand and her fingers are ice.

'No,' I say, more forcefully than I mean to. 'I don't think so. Come on, we've got to go. Now.'

We start out across the field. The earth is churned into deep grooves and clods of mud stick to our shoes, slowing us down. We head for the road and the lights in the distance.

We're doing OK until I look behind me for Sophy, then I lose my footing in the mud and crash into a twisted tree stump. I'm doing my best not to howl when Sophy cries out for me and a minute later a flashlight swings across the field and catches us.

My shin feels sticky under my jeans. She helps me up and we go on. The rain's coming at us in angry waves. They're on us now – I look back and see them picking their way round the edge of the field, torch beams grazing the ground, their faces appearing now and again like ghosts.

A hundred feet and we'll be at the road.

Fifty feet.

Thick wet clay.

Sophy's ahead of me now. I'm feeling sick and lightheaded. I stumble again. She stops, comes back and hauls me up. 'Come on. Ben, *please!* Come on!'

The low drone of traffic ahead gets me going again. We go on our hands and knees to avoid being seen and soon we reach the ridge that borders the road. It's about six feet up but we do it. There's a gap in the traffic and we cross four lanes at speed. My chest is heaving when we stop, and already Sophy's standing with her arm out, looking for a lift.

There's a man standing by a car across the road, a way up from us.

The rain distorts his figure but I can see his face in the headlights: broad and white, his eyes black holes. He's gesticulating and saying something: shouting at us – to us – but the sound is lost in the traffic and the wind. He looks over our heads just as a car pulls up and offers us a lift.

As we move off, I take Sophy's hand in mine and I hold on like I'm drowning. I look back but the man's gone.

I call Dick from the car and he meets us on the ring road near home.

'Your phones.'

'What?'

'Your phones? Did you have them turned on?'

We look at each other.

'Yes,' we say slowly.

He looks over his shoulder at us. 'That's how they

found you. GPS on these phones – they can track
you anyplace. My bad – should have thought of that
– should have said. Turn them off now. You can use
this.' He throws a scratched mobile onto my lap. 'My
number's in it.'

'They tracked our phones?' says Sophy. 'Jesus, Ben.'

'Course they did. That's what they do,' he says, and
to me, 'You turned it off?'

'I – Yeah. Yeah.'

I slump back in the seat rubbing my leg, and he says,
'So, I had a look at the memory card.'

'Yeah?' I say.

'Nothing – just a line of text.'

'A line?'

'It said something about being on a journey … and
being lost. In dark woods, something about having
lost the right road. Mean anything to you? Something
about your dad?'

I shake my head.

'What about you? You seem like you're intelligent,'
he says to Sophy. She's been leaning on my shoulder
but she sits up.

'What's the exact line? Maybe it's an acronym?'

'Tried that, doesn't make sense. OK. I remember
it. It's not hard. It says: *Midway on our life's journey, I
found myself in dark woods, the right road lost.* I thought
maybe it was something to do with your Red Gull but
I drew a blank there too. Nothing's fitting together at
the moment but it will. It will. I'm hopeful.'

She leans back against me. The weight of her, her skin on mine makes me want her all over again. The sun's coming up and streaks of red are threaded across the sky as we head through and out of town.

Dick drives about half a mile up the London Road, then turns down a narrow alley. The wing mirrors buckle against the brickwork. It opens out after that and we bump and jerk to a standstill, outside a row of lock-ups.

A familiar figure is waiting.

Maurice.

He's standing outside an open garage and guides the car in as Dick reverses. When we've all squeezed out, he shakes hands with Dick and gives me a friendly pat on the back.

'You look a sight, mate – mud bath, eh?' He nods at Sophy and says to me, 'You're a dark horse ain't you, you bugger? I'm rattling on about my lady love and he don't say nothing about this one. I'm Maurice.'

Sophy says, 'Hi.'

I say, 'Maurice, what are you doing here?'

He looks surprised. 'This is my place. The Dick's asked me to mobilise my peeps on The Grid. I've got them working on your case.'

I look at him blankly and Dick says, 'The Grid – Second Life. That's what they call it. The Grid. Maurice is big in Second Life. He knows a lot of people. Conspiracy theorists, journos, private investigators. People can network there – ask questions – in relative privacy.'

'Oh. Right.'

'Yeah,' says Maurice rubbing his hands together, 'I've put the call out. Red Gull?'

I nod slowly.

'There's a lot of computer whizzos on The Grid,' says Maurice. 'If it's out there, they'll find it. I never knew you knew the Dick. I never knew your dad was one of these scientists, either. I've been reading about it. Who's hungry?'

I almost put my hand up. Maurice opens a gate opposite the lock-up, and leads us through a dank, weedy garden up some steps to a door. There are grilles on the windows and across the door, and while we watch him open up, I can feel Sophy's hand, curled like a shell in mine.

Inside it's gloomy. We're standing in a small narrow kitchen that looks through into a living room. The floors are covered in clothes, dishes, pizza boxes. A fat bluebottle tiptoes across a pile of plates in the sink. There's a smell: a heavy, cloying, musky smell that I can't quite place until I meet it. An old Alsatian heaves itself off the sofa, puts its head in my crotch, sniffs, then wanders about between us, brushing up clouds of hair and dust. Maurice gives it a pat and waves an empty pizza box at us.

'Make yourselves comfy,' he calls. We look at each other. There's the sofa of course and a table. But everything is covered in stuff: piled up in doorways, leaning against the legs of furniture, on window sills.

We stand and steam by the radiator and pick off the worst of the mud.

Later, after we've eaten, Maurice moves a stack of unwashed dishes from the kitchen counter into the sink and fires up his laptop. He attaches headphones and mic and leans in, wiping his hands on his trousers. 'Let's see what's going on.'

And there it is. The rear view of Maurice's Avatar: a sleek, muscled back in a ripped T-shirt, firm buttocks under tight leather trousers and … webbed feet. On his head he has a kind of bony crest in bright green and, hovering above it, a little caption with a name. 'This is Mo,' he says.

'Cool,' says Sophy, 'who's he supposed to be?'

Maurice looks puzzled for a moment then he says brightly, 'He's me.'

'Oh! Oh right,' she says and bends quickly to pat the dog.

'Right. Here he comes. This is Johnno. I'm hoping he may have something for us.'

And then Maurice does the voice, the 'Mo' voice. It's so funny, I have to go into a corner and pretend to have a coughing fit. It's a kind of mid-Atlantic growl. 'Johnno, my man, how you doing? Did you get anywhere?'

Johnno is a Schwarzenegger-type, really built and wearing a black boiler suit. 'Not here,' he says.

'Earwigs,' says Maurice to me. 'Thought as much.' Then to Johnno, 'IMS?'

'IMS.'

He peels off the headphones and starts typing.

Go.

Rees Global looks great from the outside. Tricksy to get much on them but people have been digging around this for a while.

So?

Arteries.

???

I watch as the words spill themselves onto the screen.

Networks: all sorts. All over. We don't know how yet but we do know they're connected to the Manon Oliver Group — private Swiss bank in deep with any number of dodgy regimes with some serious human rights issues: North Korea, Libya, Zimbabwe. They're bank rolling their defence budgets (nuclear in some cases — buying uranium on the open market …) but there's other ways to make weapons. Dr C. was leading a research team at one point working on developing new resistant strains of viruses and weaponising them. Germ warfare: that's where the big money is: lower risk/higher reward.

'Wow,' squeaks Maurice. I close my eyes. My head's hurting. I feel raw — skinned — and yet totally disconnected from it all at the same time.

I have him as working on yellow fever for starters but that was a while ago — he dropped off the radar for a time. I think he was working on other stuff.

Maurice glances at me, then back at the screen, and starts to type. He leans right over the screen and I know he doesn't want me to see but I do: *So why kill him?*

You know he wasn't the only one? Deaths made to look like suicides. Want my educated guess?

Go on.

We wait.

Say you run a company that's making biological weaponry and selling it to rogue states through a middle-man. Highly illegal and if your cover is as a legit pharma company, you're not going to want anyone finding out about you. Maybe a disgruntled employee, or someone who's woken up one day with a conscience, decides to grass you to the authorities. What are you going to do? He'll start the ball rolling and then others will decide to do the same, which is pretty much what it looks like. The stakes are HUGE. You're going to burn. What are a few lives compared to what you stand to lose?

Yh, Maurice types. I'm reeling.

Maybe Dr C. decided to shop Rees. He had the goods on them and they knew it. And once they knew it, he was toast. It's just a theory but …

He ends on the dots, cursor flickering.

'So what are they looking for then?' I say, and everyone turns to look at me. 'I mean, if they … if they killed him, they got what they wanted, didn't they?'

'Clearly not,' says Dick softly.

There's quiet.

'Wowser,' says Maurice and then types to Johnno, *Anything on Red Gull?*

Nothing. Drew a complete blank on that one. But that line you gave me: 'Midway on our life's journey, I found myself in dark woods, the right road lost.' It's from Dante.

Dante?

He was a poet. 14th century.

What does it mean?

IDK. But I'll get back to you.

Maurice signs off and turns to me. 'Well. Dante. What's it about?'

I shrug. 'No idea.'

'It's a poem,' says Sophy, 'a long poem, about Heaven and Hell.'

'Oh right,' says Maurice blankly. 'He liked him, did he – your dad? Bit of a fan?'

I wake up. 'Don't know. Never heard of him till just now.'

There's an awkward silence in the room until I say, 'I'm going home.'

I catch Dick giving Maurice a look and Maurice pulls in his cheeks. 'I don't think that's such a good –'

'You're crazy,' says Dick. 'What did you not understand about all of this?'

'I don't care. Just take us home.'

Maurice says, 'Stay here?'

We all look at him. Dick says, 'You could –'

I hear myself say, 'Could *what*? They found us in your so-called safe house in a few hours. To be honest, I don't *feel* safe anywhere right now so I might as well be doing that at home as anywhere else.'

I'm breathing hard, and Maurice pads over, rubs me on the back and says gently, 'Listen mate, you've been up all night, you're filthy. Just have a shower and a kip here and we'll talk about it later. How's that?'

I look at Sophy who sits down. 'Good idea,' she says.

I breathe out a bit. Dick grunts at no one in particular, and Maurice puts his headphones back on.

16

In the end, we sleep till seven in the evening, and then Dick drives us back to my place. He doesn't want to but I make him.

I'm in the kitchen with him when Sophy comes in. 'I think we should go to the police,' she says.

'No,' says Dick.

'*No?*' she says, 'just *no*? Why not?'

He sighs and I hear a slight rattle under his breath. 'It's like Ben said, there's no proof. What are you going to tell 'em? What are you going to say? "Aw, we found this line from Dante on a memory card, we think it's something to do with Rees Global and all those deaths and germ-warfare"…' He looks from her to me and shakes his head violently, making his jowls shudder.

She lowers her head, then looks at me. 'What do you think?'

I say, 'I guess he's right. We have to do more. We have to find what they're looking for before they do.

Whatever it was my dad left when he died.'

Dick nods. 'That's it. Because right now, all you've got are some loony-tunes conspiracy theories from people like me. Leave it a while. We need to do some more digging, get something more concrete. Ben, can I talk to you? In *private*?'

Sophy glares at him and folds her arms. He ushers me out of the kitchen into the hall and, without taking his eyes off me, reaches into his jacket and pulls out something bound in a handkerchief. Magician-like, he whisks off the cover and there, on his outstretched palm, is a gun.

'Dick, *what the fuck?*'

'It's a Colt. Handy little piece. Keep you safe. It's loaded. You know how to use it?'

He pushes it at me and I feel the press of its cold weight in my hand for a moment before I give it back to him. 'For Christ's sake, Dick, this is *Surrey*, not Mexico City. What you giving me a *gun* for?'

He fixes me with his piglet eyes and says quietly, 'These guys Ben. You don't *know* these guys yet? *After all this?* Come on. Think about it.'

I remember Sophy by the mermaid and I nearly take it but sense gets the better of me. 'No mate, you hang on to it. Seriously. I cannot deal. Not with a gun as well as all the rest of it.'

He looks peeved. 'If you say so. Listen, I got to bounce. Goodbye Sophy,' he calls. 'You get some rest. And,' he whispers to me, 'try and stay together.'

He leaves in a hurry.

Back in the kitchen, she's putting on her coat. 'What was all that about?' she says, heading for the door.

'Tell you later. Where are you going?'

'Home,' she says.

'Please don't.'

'I want to. You can't stop me.'

'Of course I can't *stop* you. What do you think I *am*? I just … I think we'll be safer if we … Dick says –'

'*Dick says* … you're pathetic. I don't know what I –' and she stops herself before she says what we both know she was going to say. 'Sorry. Look, just let me go, OK? I'll be OK.'

I reckon I've got one last plea in me before I give up altogether.

'*Please* Sophy? *Stay*. You told your Mum you were away. No one's expecting you back. It's not safe … it's … you know Dick was trying to give me a gun back there?'

'Oh my God, Ben, are you *actually* mad?'

'No. No. I didn't take it but I reckon he's right. Look, I don't know what they want, I really don't but … and I'm not saying I'm … I know I'm nothing special but I think we should maybe stick together.' I look at her. '*Sophy?*'

There's a long pause and I feel the room getting smaller, and then she lets her coat slide off her shoulders and I take it from her. She stands in front of me then, in the middle of the room and we're stopped like a broken clock.

She shrugs.

'You want something to eat?' I say.

'No thanks.'

'Watch TV?'

'No.'

'You mind if I eat something?'

'Go ahead.'

The conversation splinters and snaps after that and she takes herself off to the living room while I microwave a bowl of beans. I hear her padding from room to room, a shoulder on the door jamb, the turn of a handle. I can feel her too. Close. Feel the house filling up with her.

I'm troughing on the beans over the sink when she comes in.

'Ben?' I turn and she's holding a book: leather bound with sharp gilt tooling on the spine, one of my father's. It's open on the flyleaf.

I peer at it. 'What?'

There's a watercolour picture of a garden with a fountain and a fan of decorative rills running away from it. In ink beside it, is written:'*For David, with best wishes, A.*'

'*A*? You mean A, like who is *A?*' I say. 'I have no −'

'*No.* Look. On the other side.' And there it is, on the inside of the cover, a red ink stamp, slightly faded and rubbed at the edges but unmistakeable: *RED GULL BOOKSHOP.*

Slowly, I take the book from her hands and put it on the table next to the beans and I lean in and wrap my arms around her. 'You're a genius.'

She smiles. A little. 'I know.'

'Come on.'

I race up to my room with Sophy at my heels, grab my laptop and we look for it online. There's no website, only a Yellow Pages address: *Red Gull Bookshop. 125 Charing Cross Road WC2 7JW. Specialist Garden Design History. Open seven days a week: 10.00am to 6.00pm. Proprietor, Mr Ambrose Bellamy.*

'Ambrose. That's the "A" maybe?'

'I'm going to go there. Find out,' I say.

'What, *now?*' she says.

'Tomorrow. I'll go tomorrow.'

'I'll come with you if you like.'

'*Really?*' I say, and try not to sound as pleased as I feel.

'Why not?'

And is it right? Here and now, with my breath smelling of baked beans? Would it be right to do what I want to do and kiss her? Everything's got so mixed up with us. When did we turn into Batman and Robin when all I ever wanted was for her to be my girlfriend? She's sitting on the bed next to me, so close our thighs are touching and it's like a burn.

I look away, give my mouth a quick once-round with my tongue, and edge my hand a little closer to hers.

Then she says, 'Can I just check my Facebook?'

And the whole tower block of me is ignited and explodes and falls gracefully to the ground in a haze of thick dust. 'Go ahead,' I say.

She takes the laptop and just when things couldn't get much worse, I see that cock Darren's face up there and a message.

I get up then and go to the door. 'Just going to get something to eat.'

She looks up and says, 'You just ate didn't you?'

Fuck. 'Yeah. Yeah I did, I forgot. Yeah.' I turn on the TV, go back to the bed, sit down way away at the other end and pull out my Xbox controller.

Sophy goes to say something but the sound of gunfire and mortar fills the room and I'm lobbing bullets at terrorists. There's something about gaming that stops you caring or wanting anything else. They should have it on prescription at the doctor's. Once I'm into the game, the room and the rest of the world goes out of focus for a while. Even *I* go out of focus and all I am is two hands and a gun sight. And that's enough for me.

After a while – and I really couldn't say how long – she comes right up to me and says, 'I'm really tired.'

I don't look up but I nod.

'*Ben?*'

'Mmm?'

'Can you … pause that for a minute?' she asks and I do, and I'm back in the room with her, except now it feels like Darren's right in there with us.

'Where can I sleep?' she says. And suddenly there's her in the gas light in Dick's burrow, and I'm pulling off her top, and seeing her bright skin and the hollows and curves of her …

I kill the game and put down the controller; stand up, then sit back down, make my voice come out soft. 'Er … here. You can sleep here if you …'

Mistake. BIG mistake – should *so* not have suggested that. A kind of blank expression crosses her face and then she just looks annoyed. Why can't I get it *right*? *Ever*?

'Or … there's Charlie's room. Across the hall. The bed's still made. No. I mean I'll change the sheets and –'

'It's OK. Charlie's room's fine. Thanks. I'll just get a glass of water.'

'Do you want …?'

'It's all right. You can go back to your game now.'

I hear her on the stairs, and I go and look in my mirror. *Moron*, I say to myself, *It's late. It's dark. You're alone with this girl. In your room. On a BED. And the best thing you can come up with, the very best, is to get out your fucking Xbox.*

She's back upstairs now and I hear her footsteps stop for a second outside my door. Then a minute later, I hear the door to Charlie's room close.

I go downstairs, bring up some beers, and play on for hours. It's gone one o'clock when I turn off the game and lie down.

For ages, I trawl between sleep and waking, where faces, pale and indistinct, wash in and out. I'm drifting anchorless in weeds that are red like Sophy's hair. When I finally get to sleep, I have the strangest dream.

I'm walking through a dark wood full of twisted, tangled trees. And as I go further in, their branches brush and claw at me. In the distance, there's a light, dim at first but getting brighter, and as I walk towards it, I can see my father. As I get closer, I see he has no eyes. In their place are deep dark pits. He's shouting but I can't make out the words. He's standing on a crossroads in the middle of the wood, and he turns and walks away down a path that leads to blackness, and I want to run after him, to save him, but the trees curl themselves around me and I can't get free.

I wake up to Sophy standing over me, fully dressed, pulling on my arm.

'There's someone in the house.'

17

It's six in the morning and she's right. There are footsteps coming up the stairs. I hear the spring and the creak across the landing, and a bolt of panic drives up my spine like a roman candle. I jump up.

'Get under the bed!'

'*Don't be stupid,*' she spits back.

I'm looking around me when the handle turns and a torch light yawns into the room. I can feel her hand on my arm.

'Hello again,' says a voice. I can't see him because the beam from the torch is blinding but I know it. It's the American from the Bentley. From Rees.

He lowers the torch and I can see him now: tall and thin with those fuzzy grey eyes. I can smell onion on his breath from here. The muscles in my neck pinch.

'Hi there,' he says to Sophy. He looks her up and down and nods with a half-approving sneer that makes me want to drive a garden rake through his eyeballs.

'Piss off,' she says. He takes a step towards her.

'What do you want?' I say.

'Sit down please,' he says and we sit down on the bed. I can hear her breath coming in shallow gasps.

He bends over the bed. He's wearing gloves and he takes my chin in one hand and lifts my face. I can feel that familiar tightening in my throat and the ants marching round the inside of my skull, and I want to hit him but I'm worried about Sophy and what she'll think.

'You know what we want Ben,' he says quietly. I sit and stare at the floor and ball my fists till my knuckles hurt. 'Listen,' he makes it slow. 'For the last time: your dad, David Collins, took something from us. Something that wasn't his to take.' I notice his right pocket belly out with the shape of something heavy. 'Are you *listening* to me, Ben?'

Close up, his breath reeks. I shake my head violently but I have no words. No voice. Outside, the grey wash of dawn is breaking the dark.

He goes on. 'Let's all stay calm. You see, commitment is important in our business – has to be – and Dr Collins dropped out of the programme. He let us down. Before he died, he took some material that belonged to us. A lot of important, sensitive information pertaining to the work we do. It was appropriated, *stolen* by your father. We just want it back, that's all. Now, he was a smart guy. He wasn't going to just hide this away without telling someone and I think you know where it is. Am I right?'

'I don't know what you're talking about.'

'What about you?' he says to Sophy.

'Leave her out of it. She doesn't know anything.'

'*Out of it?*' he repeats. '*Out of it?* Well, if I'm going to leave her *out of it*, then what is *it* I'm leaving her out of? Does that mean you're *in* it?'

'Fuck off and die.'

'OK Ben, I didn't want to go there but let's think about this. There are other people involved here, people you care about. Your brother for one.'

'What about my brother?'

'*What about your brother*? Come on Ben, you're not *that* stupid. Do I have to spell it out for you? All I'm saying is it would be better for everyone if you give us what we want. You know, simpler. For. Everyone.' And he looks at Sophy. 'I'm only saying you wouldn't want anyone to get hurt.'

'We don't know anything,' says Sophy, 'just leave us alone.'

'Listen honey,' he says sweetly, 'let me tell you something, you interrupt me again and I *will* hurt you. You understand?'

I stand up and go to grab his arm but he throws me back. Sophy sits very still and upright on the bed.

'Don't touch her. Don't touch her!'

'Come on Ben. Just give it up and I'll go. What did he tell you? What did you find out? Where is it?'

I look straight at him and I give him the finger. And then it all happens very quickly.

He pulls me up by my T-shirt and punches me in my gut so hard that all the breath is knocked out of me. The pain is intense: it's like someone's taken every internal organ out, wrung them under boiling water and pushed them back in again. It takes me a while to get myself together to swivel round and face Sophy. Her face is white and her eyes are full.

'I'm OK, Sophy,' I say. 'It's OK.'

I try to catch her eye but she's staring straight ahead. He looks at me and then at her and very calmly hits her across the face.

'Leave her alone!' I push up and aim a fist at him but I'm still winded from where he hit me.

'Tell me about your dad.'

Sophy's eyes are wide and she's shaking her head. He turns back to her, pinches her face in one hand and pulls back her hair with the other.

'Leave her alone! *Leave her alone!*'

He shoves her back, then he leans over me. 'Ben … it's easy.'

I try to sit up again. 'I don't know anything. Why didn't you ask him before you *killed* him?'

He looks at me, says, 'What makes you think we killed him?'

'Fuck you.'

He grabs hold of Sophy's arm then and twists it. I see her flinch in pain, and again I try to haul myself up. 'Let go of her!'

He stamps me back with his boot. 'Or what?' he says

as he tightens his grip on her. She gasps.

'*Leave her! Let go of her!*'

Still holding her, he says to me, 'Let's be clear about this, Ben. If you want me to *stop* doing what I'm doing, you're going to have to talk to me.'

Sophy's shaking her head again. He turns back to her. 'Ah look. I think she wants some more.'

'*No!* No! OK. OK.'

'That's better. I'm listening.'

'It's nothing. Just a line.'

He lets go of her and her head rocks forward. She inhales sharply. I feel sick that I'm the cause of this. Me and my insane ideas about messing with something much, much more powerful than we were. Who did I think I was, Tom Cruise? I'm just some stupid kid who's way out of his depth.

'A line?'

'Something from out of Dante.'

'Go on.'

I say, 'Something about being lost in the dark woods … midway on life's journey … er … I found myself alone …'

'You're kidding, right?'

'No.'

'What does it mean?'

'I don't know. It's all there was.'

'A code?' He sounds like he's thinking aloud. Then, 'Where did you find it? Did your dad tell you?'

The house is silent. The walls of the room seem to

close in on us. 'A memory card. We ... I found it in his desk.'

'So this line from Dante was on the card. What else?'

'Nothing, I swear.'

'You're lying.'

'No! I ...'

'Don't fuck with me, Ben.'

I take a breath. 'Red Gull.'

'*No, Ben!*' Sophy cries.

He turns quickly. 'Red Gull? What is that?'

'*Find the Red Gull.* That's all I know.'

'What is a Red Gull? Some kind of sea bird? What's that?'

And he and I are so locked in, that what happens next is a complete surprise to both of us. The first thing I hear is a loud hammering coming up the stairs, then a dark figure, his face in shadow. The American twists around in confusion, and in that moment I see my chance. There's an empty beer bottle by the bed. Without thinking, I grab it and bring it down across the side of his head. The American sways back, his knees buckle and he falls. In the half light, I see a dark run of blood winding its way across his face.

Behind him, the figure pushes back his hoodie and a bright rash of pimples shows in the dawn light. 'Ben, what the fuck?'

'Sam?' I say.

'Hi,' he says to Sophy.

'What are you doing here?' I say.

'Party,' he says. 'In Vauxhall. Club. Got the early train back and I wondered if you were up. I'm wired, man. I took something. Can't go to sleep. So I thought –'

'Sam, mate, I can't –'

'Is this for real?' he says, pointing at the American. 'This guy? What's going on?'

'Yeah. It's for real. Listen mate. Seriously. Thanks. But we've got to go.'

'Well I'm not staying here with him,' he says.

'Course not.'

'Come on!' Sophy says. 'Quick.'

As I get to my feet, the pain in my guts stabs at me but I ignore it and grab my clothes. The American groans and reaches out blindly.

It's light now. Sam's already on the stairs. Sophy's next to me.

We look at each other.

18

We're in the kitchen and I can hear muffled sounds coming from upstairs.

'Should we call the police?' says Sophy.

'What?' I say, grinding my feet into my trainers. 'No. We just need to get going.'

'But he's coming round … he'll be …'

'I know.' I hesitate for just a second, and in that second I go through a list of the things I'd like to do to him to silence him for good. Then I rouse myself, grab my jacket, and say, 'Which is why we need to move.'

Sam's waiting by the front door. 'Sound. Come on.'

We go out of the house and down the quiet street where overhanging trees drip and blow, turn into the main road and head down the hill into town. We don't speak. All I can hear is my breathing over Sophy's breathing and hers over mine and my feet on tarmac.

Once we're on the London Road, I say to Sam, 'Thanks mate, we can take it from here.'

'No way,' he says. His eyes are glowing. 'I'm in, mate. Whatever. I'm coming.'

'Can't. You don't want to get caught up,' I say, 'seriously.'

Sophy puts a hand on his arm. 'We'll tell you all about it later. Promise.'

'Yeah but –'

'Sam, you're going to crash,' I say. 'Any minute now. I know you. Get yourself home. I'll come round later.'

He staggers and backs into a tree. 'Yeah. Yeah maybe. Cool.'

'Thanks again,' I say.

We go straight to Maurice's place and bang on the door.

'Bugger me. What's up my friend?' he says, 'you look like a bloody orc,' and to Sophy, 'hello darling.'

'Been running,' I say.

'Right.' He nods sagely. 'Right.' And just when I think he's not going to ask any questions, he says to Sophy, 'You *all right* love?' There's a mark across her face where the American hit her, and guilt smacks into me like a wrecking ball. She nods and smiles. He puts the kettle on and opens a biscuit tin. I start to tell him what happened.

'One of them – the guys from Rees – came to my house.'

'Ooh. Nasty. And ...?'

'It's like before, they say my dad took something. *Stole* something from them. They want it back.'

'You've been warned mate. You got to be careful. What did you tell him? Have a Jaffa. Hope you're all right with them. I'm out of gingers.'

'I told him …'

'What?'

'About the Dante.'

'*And?*'

'The Red Gull.'

'Well, that's all right. He won't be able to make any more sense out of that than we can,' he says. But something tells me he's not convinced. I'm about to tell him what we found out about Red Gull when he says, 'Your dad – I had a little nose around the web.'

The muscle-bound avatars spring into my head and hover. 'Yeah?' I say.

'I looked him up. Quite a bit on there about him.'

'I know.'

He totters back and leans against the table, brushing biscuit crumbs from his belly. In the dark fug behind him, the dog yawns and stretches. 'You heard of Aiden James?' he says, stirring tea bags in chipped mugs.

'Er … yeah. He was … I remember the name.'

'He was a journalist. He was interested in Rees and the biotech industry like lots of people – their contacts with dodgy regimes – all that. He was working on a book about it before he died. Clever chap I reckon – can't be easy digging up the dirt on these boys. As we know, they're secretive little bunnies.'

I reach for a Jaffa cake. I don't know why, I hate

them. Maurice goes on. 'You know he met your dad?'

'Really? When?'

'In Chicago, 31st March, 2013 – this year. The day before he died.'

'*You're kidding.*'

'The Maurice does not lie.' He hands us the tea. There are little scabs and peelings of milk floating on the surface.

'So … he might …'

'He might nothing, mate. The man's dead.'

'Yeah but –'

'It must be connected though. Maybe he had something off your dad? What do you think? Papers? Research? Some kind of dirt?'

'Maybe,' I say.

'Maybe that's what the Red Gull is about? Like a code name or something? Like in the War?' Sophy shakes her head. 'We *know* what the Red Gull is,' she says.

He puts down his mug and leans in. 'Go on, darling.'

'It's a bookshop. In London.'

'It never is,' he says.

'Maurice,' I say. 'What day is it?'

'No idea, mate.'

'Can you lend us some money?'

'No problemo.'

He shuffles about under papers and rotting food and comes up with a handful of greasy notes. He screws them into a ball and presses them into my hand. I peel off a couple of twenties and give the rest back to him.

'It's OK. We just need a return to London.'

He pushes the money back at me. 'Keep it. You never know, my friend.' Then he says darkly, 'You can give it back if you don't use it in the fleshpots.'

'Thanks.'

'Are you going now then? I'll give you a lift to the station. Just put my trousers on. Stay, boy!' he shouts at the dog, who slumps back onto the floor.

'No need Maurice. We're OK ...'

'Just hang on a mo,' he calls. 'Make yourself at home. Mi casa es su casa.'

While he's out of the room and the dog is watching us with lazy eyes, Sophy comes over to me, right up close, and she looks up at me but all I see is the dark weal on her cheek. I hold her face in my hands and I feel her fill me up.

'I'm sorry,' I say because any more is impossible.

She shakes her head. I feel her jaw twist and I see the white line of her throat. 'Ben. I just want ...'

Then Maurice comes back in. Perfect timing. He's wearing a maroon tracksuit about two sizes too small. 'Let's go,' he says.

We just make the 8.35 to Waterloo, squashed in with hundreds of bodies all smelling of deodorant, and then get the underground to Leicester Square. It's a quarter to ten when we come out onto Charing Cross Road.

The big cinema signs tower over the Square: the Odeon, the Empire. There are fast food places everywhere: ice cream, burgers, fried chicken. A tramp roots in a bin near me and pulls out a half-eaten sandwich. We lean against a wall and I roll a cigarette and watch a one-legged pigeon hopping from table to table outside a café. A party of foreign kids with matching backpacks go past. At ten o'clock I drop my smoke and we move.

Charing Cross Road at that end is full of second-hand bookshops selling anything from antique maps to Victorian porn. We find Red Gull easily. It's on the corner of a cobbled alleyway that backs onto a theatre on the other side. In the window, there's a moth-eaten velvet cloth on which someone has placed an open book, very old and full of dense text and so thick with dust you can't make out the words. There's no sign over the shop, just a number. In the window, next to the book, is one of those aluminium plates you get that say *Manager's Office* or *No Junk Mail*. That's it.

Red Gull Bookshop.

19

Sophy pushes the door. A clock on the wall above the door is just finishing its chime as we enter. The room is small but it feels smaller because every inch of space is full of books: books in glass cases and on shelves and piled up on the floor. It's like they've been here so long, you can almost hear them: a kind of heavy, breathy rustle. There's just a little pathway through them up to the cash desk.

The walls above the shelves are hung with scratchy oil paintings and old photographs of weird family groups. In among them there's a boar's head with curving tusks. At the back, over a small door, is a long tribal spear decorated with feathers. The place has a kind of gingery smell of old leather and mould. I'm still getting used to the dim in here after the brightness of the street and I'm startled when I hear a voice next to us.

'Can I help you?' A throaty Irish rasp just behind my left shoulder.

'Um.' I pick up a large leather-bound book called *The Esoteric Structure of Late Medieval Physic Gardens*. 'Do you have anything on … er …Victorian gardens?'

He comes round to face us. Dark, closing eyes and a nose like a root vegetable from which purple veins sprout and spider over his cheeks. 'No.'

'Oh … right.'

He leans in, takes the book from me and holds it against his chest, releasing a little puff of dust as he does so. He coughs and says, 'Well.'

There's something kind of familiar about him. Sophy steps up. 'Are you Ambrose Bellamy?'

He raises two whiskery eyebrows. 'That's me.'

'We're here about … about …' and she looks at me and I finish.

'My dad.'

'I know.'

I stare at him. 'Sorry?'

'That's all right,' he says, calm as anything. 'Go on.' Still holding on to the book, he cocks his head to one side and hooks a knob of wax out of his ear with a pencil.

I stumble on. 'Um. David Collins. He died in May.'

'Yes, I heard. I'm sorry.'

Long strings of dust motes hang in the air.

'So you knew him?'

He's standing very close to me and the books on the shelves weigh in on us. Now I know I've seen him before, I just don't know where.

'That's right.'

I take a breath. 'So ... things have been a bit weird lately ... and –'

'A bit weird?'

He pinches the knob of wax in between his thumb and forefinger and rolls it around.

'Yeah, lots of things. And er ... one of the things is ... the reason I'm here ... the other day I got this note and it said ...'

'Find the Red Gull?'

I hear Sophy gasp behind me. He goes on. '*Trust no one? Tell no one?* You didn't quite not tell anyone, did you?' He looks hard at Sophy.

'What the ...? How did you ...? What ...?'

'Because I wrote it, that's how.'

He smiles and the tip of his tongue pokes out between dry lips like a snake's. Now I know. He's the man who was waving at us from across the road when we were running from Dick's barn: the white anxious face and the dark eyes. We're still standing facing each other in the passageway when the bell makes me jump.

A tall woman in a kind of cloak comes in. 'Hello dear, is it in yet?' she says.

'Not yet Jean, I'll let you know. I'm just having to close up for a bit.'

He puts the book to one side, gives it a kind of affectionate little pat as he places it on the top of another pile. Then he squeezes past us, sees her gently out of the shop, bolts the door, twists the *open* sign around, then turns to face me. He looks serious. 'A long

time ago your father asked me to ... take an interest.
I was –'

'That night on the road by the farm? In the rain?
That was you?'

He picks and pinches at his chin, fixes his eyes on
me. There's a sour reek of drink hanging about him.
'That was me.'

'How did you know we were there?'

'How do you think? Because I followed you and I
followed them. I was in your road too – in the car. I
didn't want to alarm you outright but ... your father
– he knew they'd be coming for you, you see. Once
your brother had left ... they've been waiting, watching.
You were – *are* – vulnerable. So I sort of, well – I did
what I could.'

I swallow air. 'He asked you to look out for me?
When?'

'Oh, a good while ago. He said if anything happened
to him to keep an eye on you.'

Sophy coughs, says, 'So he knew Rees were after him?'

He only smiles.

'Why didn't you just come and tell me? Say, *Hey,
Ben, I'm at the Red Gull bookshop* instead of all this
mysterious shit?'

He doesn't answer straight away and I don't even
notice till after he's finished that I'm holding my breath.

'Maybe it wasn't fair,' he says, 'maybe I should have
... I don't know, *revealed* myself sooner. I didn't know
then – should have, didn't – just quite what they were

capable of. And I thought you'd know – I figured his nibs might have mentioned the shop.'

'No.'

'Clearly. If it had taken you any longer I would have done something.'

'They want something from my dad, something he took, stole, hid, I don't know … they threatened me. They –'

'I know. I know now.'

'So why *Find the Red Gull*? Why come here?' asks Sophy a bit too loudly.

'Because …' he breathes, 'because –'

'That line on the memory card?' I say. 'You put that there too?'

'What memory card?'

'Don't bullshit me.'

'I have literally no idea what you're talking about.'

'Midway on our life's journey, I found myself in dark woods, the right road lost.'

'Dante.'

'Yeah.'

'First Canto. Pinsky translation, bit modern for your Pa but good all the same.'

'OK.'

'He liked Dante.'

For some reason, an image snaps into my head: my father. He's sitting at the breakfast table scoring the top off a soft-boiled egg in front of him and as I watch, he picks the shell off delicately, piece by tiny piece, till the white dome is left glistening and unbroken in the cup. He's smiling to himself.

'Does it mean anything to you?' Sophy asks him.

He shakes his head. 'Nothing. At least nothing significant. But, listen. I have something I need to –'

'Then what ...?' I rub my face.

'Your father knew – and you will certainly know now – some of what Rees are about, about the methods they use to get what they want. That line must be a ... a code, a trail, a secret, something only you would have known about.'

'Er ... except I don't. I'd never even heard of Dante till this came up.'

'OK. Well ...' He runs a long finger back and forth across the bridge of his nose, looks away toward the door behind us before he goes on. 'Dante was a poet. In Italy, in the fourteenth century. He wrote *The Divine Comedy*, considered to be one of the greatest literary works of the age – indeed of any age. It describes his travels through Hell, Purgatory and Heaven. It's roughly fourteen thousand lines long and it's split into three sections: Inferno, which, of course, is Hell and that's where your line comes from; Purgatorio, Purgatory, a kind of limbo – or staging post between Heaven and Hell; and Paradiso, Paradise, or Heaven. It's allegorical of course.'

He sees the blank look on my face. 'Allegorical – that means, you know, symbolic. It's an allegory of the soul's journey after death.'

'OK.'

'Mmm ... yes. And you're sure none of this means anything to you?'

'I told you.'

'Then it must be something to do with you,' Sophy says, looking straight at him.

'*Me?*' he says. 'It's got nothing to do with me. But that's not why you're here ... except, maybe ... where did you find it, the card?'

'It was hidden in his desk at home.'

He pins me again with those dog eyes, lowers his voice. 'You know, Ben, you were very special to your Pa.'

His words circle in my ears, spiral down through their coils and lick their way around the inside of my brain. The idea of Dad talking to someone about me, carrying me in his thoughts. And I'm thinking this when Ambrose says, 'Very special.'

I shrug and say nothing and look down at his feet. He's wearing slippers. I step back into a row of journals and he takes a step towards me and he sighs and it comes out like an airy whistle. The clock chimes again, breaking into the quiet.

'Do you have a copy? Of the book?' says Sophy.

He claps his hands together, says, 'Right, OK. Yes. Let's do this first. Let's have a look. Go straight to the horse's mouth, so to speak. I wonder – I have a very old copy of the Inferno with the Doré illustrations: 1868. I know he rather coveted it.'

He backs up into a musty corner where there's a table piled high with books, some so old that their

corners are curled and frothy with mould. Behind the
table are a rickety chair and a small stool. He squeezes
round, sits down and disappears behind the pile. A
hand emerges and beckons us over. Sophy sits on the
stool facing him, and I lean over the table, breathing
old leather.

'Not here, not here …' he says to himself. He gets up,
goes off down a narrow aisle between the shelves, and
comes back with a large volume and settles himself back
in the chair. The pages are thick, velvety-looking and
bound to each other with thin cord. He hums to himself
as he turns them, holds them between thumb and
forefinger. And then he stops, turns the book towards
me, smoothing back the pages with papery hands. 'First
Canto: "Nel mezzo del cammin di nostra …"'

On one side is verse in dense dark lettering, on the
other, is a gloomy engraving: a man hunched against
a thin flare of light, his robes hanging heavy about
him. Behind him a dark forest looms and at his feet,
curling upwards, a thicket of weeds seems to pull at
him. Ambrose coughs into his fist and I hear a curdling
in his throat. A ginger cat comes out from under the
table and rubs itself against my legs.

Then: '*Look*,' says Ambrose. 'Not at the picture.' He's
pointing now at the words on the facing page. Between
the lines, are faint pencil marks. 'Look,' he urges.

20

Soft grey markings dip in and out of the text and become words and when they're put together they read:

> I did not die and I did not remain alive. Think now
> for yourself, if you have any sense, what I became,
> deprived of one and of the other.

'Mmm,' he says, his finger still pushing against the page. 'That's Dante too, from the Inferno – towards the end – when Dante and his guide are in the ninth circle of Hell and they meet the King of Hell – Satan himself – waist deep in ice; the last section from the Inferno, before they go to Purgatory, you know, Limbo … where the souls sit between Hell and Heaven.'

'But what does it mean? *I didn't die and I didn't remain alive?*'

'Well – that's Purgatory – in between Heaven and Hell – he's saying he was in torment, punished … or …'

'Or what?' I say.

'Or … I don't know. I really don't. Look there's something I have to –'

But I interrupt him because I've noticed something else. Tucked deep in the groove between the bindings, and almost invisible, is a long, thin key. I reach across and gently dislodge it. It has a heart-shaped head and a furled tag, knotted with green string and on the tag, in tiny writing, is the word: *Acheron*. And on the other side of the tag: *Ben. Look in the woods.*

The sounds of traffic and people in the street seem to fade, until the only real things in the world are this shop and the book in front of us.

'Curiouser and curiouser,' says Ambrose. '*Look in the woods.*'

We turn to the book again, Ambrose's hooked finger tracing every word and every line of ink, back and forth, looking for I don't know what.

After a while I ask, 'You really didn't know this was here?'

He scores at a mark on the table with a dirty fingernail. 'No. Not this. He only said to be ready. To watch and wait and guide you here and to … Ben, if you'll just listen a moment, there's something I –'

'What's Acheron?' says Sophy.

He says, 'You've heard the term "Abandon Hope All Who Enter Here"?'

We nod.

'Oh, I remember: it's a *river*,' says Sophy, then she looks at Ambrose, 'isn't it?'

He raises an eyebrow. 'Impressive,' he says. 'It's what Dante sees written over the gates of Hell. And after you've passed through the gates, you come to a river – the river Acheron where there's a ferryman who takes the waiting souls across the river into Hell.'

'Oh.' It's all I can say. But I close my fist over the key and it warms quickly in my hand. Ambrose seems genuinely surprised. 'I had no idea about the key. He must have put it there for you to find. He knew I'd know the line from Dante – I suppose he hoped you'd do the rest.'

'That picture,' I say slowly, 'of the man – I know it. It's at home in my dad's study.' They both turn to look at me. I'm angry – boiling – but I don't know why.

Ambrose is nodding. 'He had a set of engravings. I remember him telling me.'

'And?' Sophy says.

'And nothing,' I snap. 'I'm just saying he's got that picture.'

She folds her arms and looks away.

'Woods,' says Ambrose. '*Look in the woods*. He was a card, wasn't he? Anyone have any idea what this is about?'

'The woods near your house?' Sophy leans in again.

'Those woods? What the …? What, I'm supposed to go barging about up there on my hands and knees looking for who knows what?'

She blinks, swallows and reddens, and I feel like shit. 'Sorry,' I try, 'sorry.'

She turns her head again so all I can see is her hair.

'Woods,' Ambrose is saying. He's pointing at the page. '*Woods*. What about the engraving? It has to be in that picture somewhere.'

We all turn our attention back to the book, but I can sense Sophy bristle every time I'm too close, feel the way she twists away from me.

Then I get it. 'It's back at home. It must be. When he says, *look in the woods*, that's what he must have meant.'

'I don't understand.' At least she's looking at me now.

'There must be something in that picture at home,' I say.

'In it?' says Sophy.

'In it, on it, behind it … I don't know. It has to be that, doesn't it?'

'It's possible,' says Ambrose. He closes the book sending up drifts of dust like pollen into the air. 'But Ben, I need to –'

'I've got to go,' I say. 'I want to get back and check it out.'

'Good idea.' Sophy gets up, goes and stands at the door in a prickle of book dust. I can see she's still pissed with me. I go to follow her but a hand on my arm makes me stop.

Ambrose says softly, 'Ben, wait. I've been trying to tell you – the reason you're here, the reason I brought you here – there's something I have to …' His eyes are wide and streaked with little threads of blood. His whisky breath's like jam.

Sophy is unlocking the door at the front of the shop.

'Come on then,' she says.

'Your father asked me to –'

'What?'

He takes a breath, says to Sophy, 'Why don't you go across the road, get us all a coffee?'

'But …?' she says, looking at me.

He pulls out a grubby fold of notes from his back pocket, peels off a tenner and holds it out for her. 'There's a love. Just need to have a little chat with Ben. You don't mind, do you?'

'Um … no. OK,' she says.

'I'll have a latte: three sugars. Thanks.'

She looks at me.

'Er … same,' I say because I can't think about coffee.

The bell jangles as she leaves.

'Nice girl,' he says.

'We need to go. I want to get back, see what's in the picture. I want –'

'I know. I know you do. But it can wait a bit longer.'

He threads back to the door and slides up the bolt and comes back to the table.

'What is it?' I say.

He points to the stool. 'Sit down, Ben.'

I sit down then and he comes to sit facing me. 'OK. Before we start, a bit about me: I sell books but I'm not just a bookseller, although you maybe worked that out for yourself. I work in different ways for different people, organisations. I'm discreet, I'm careful and I always get the job done.'

I look at him, his beagle eyes, the patchy beard growth, the doughy skin. 'I don't understand.'

He leans in further. 'You don't need to. All you need to know is that when someone charges me to do something, I get it done. I make it happen – and I'm not talking about first editions. I've known your father a long time, Ben – a very long time – known what he did and what he didn't do, what he wanted and what he couldn't have. I've done things for him that have hurt people, things I'm not particularly proud of, things I could probably – possibly – go to prison for – but I did them all because I believed in him – in what he wanted at the end.'

'*So?*' I'm looking past him towards the door.

He grips my wrist, raises his voice. 'Hey! Don't come it with your arrogant teenage bollocks. You want to sleep with that girl, then go ahead, I'm not stopping you – but when I ask you to listen to me, you bloody well listen, OK?'

I'm listening now.

'This is really important, Ben. It's about your dad and it's about Rees, and more than that, it's about you.'

I nod, wide-eyed.

'The reason I – *we* – got you here in the first place is because I have something for you, something from your father.'

I stare at him. 'You've got something from … What does –?'

'I'm about to tell you.'

'So the whole Dante thing – you really didn't know?'

'No idea. Complete surprise. It's perhaps connected in some way but what I have to tell you – give you – is different.'

'OK. What is it?'

'Before I give it to you, you must understand something. That he changed, he did change. He … he repented, if you like – old-fashioned word – but … well, it fits here I think.'

I wait, my fingers digging into my palms. He lowers his voice: 'You remember the injections, Ben, the blood you gave?'

I nod slowly. 'My mum had … How did you know about –?'

He cuts me off. 'Yes. But *after* your mum died? Do you know what that was all about?'

'He was working on gene therapy for cancers. When she died, he carried on. He wanted –'

I stop because he's looking at me, shaking his head. 'What I'm going to tell you was told to me in the strictest confidence. I hope you won't betray that. Even to your girl. You understand? You *promise*? You must promise me this.'

'OK. OK, yes. I promise.'

He goes on. 'At Rees your father built something – and I'm sure if he were standing here today, he'd say he bitterly regretted it but there it is. You're right, he did do some work on cancer treatments when your mother got sick, and I know you were a part of that – giving blood and so on – but … mostly, he was working on something quite, quite different. His area of interest from very early on … his specialisation was … disease: not so much curing it, as …' he falters a moment, looks away, 'as … making it. He made … he created a *virus*. From the ground up. An extraordinary … a kind of … *plague* virus – I don't know much more but … where you come in – there's no easy way to say this – later – much later – when he needed to create a vaccine, he needed a living subject to "grow" it in, and he used *you* – *your blood* – to make it and test it and –'

I'm on my feet, kicking the stool from under me. 'You *what*? How do you know this? That's bullshit! It's bullshit! Don't –' And I break off then, and stop and look at him. He's deadly serious.

'I appreciate this is hard to take in. But do you understand now why you mustn't tell anyone? I mean *anyone*.'

'What's going to happen to me? Am I going to get this disease? Have I got it? Charlie … did he …? Am I infectious? What the …?'

'No, you're not going to catch it – it's not like that. You're immune – the only one who is. And, no, I don't think Charlie was involved. But Ben, I've told you all I know – he wanted to prepare you.'

'Jesus.'

'Sit down.'

'He did that? He …' Thoughts are racing through my brain: images, words, his hands, needles, his back bent over his desk, labels, tubes and that cherry-wood box.

'He was a complicated man.'

I can feel tears coming. 'Why didn't he tell me what he was doing? Why did he –?'

'I don't know. But I do have something for you: from him.' Sophy is knocking at the door now with the coffees. He holds up a hand for her to wait, hooks a small key from his pocket and unlocks a drawer in the table. I hear the scratch of paper and he brings out a brown envelope with a window at the front and slides it into my hands. I look up at him.

He nods. 'Open it.'

Inside, is a hand-written letter to me from my father.

Dear Ben

If you are reading this it means that you are with Ambrose. That's good.

I have left this in his care. You can trust him. He will tell you what you need to know but it is very important to me that you and only you are involved from this point on.

You may know by now a little about my work. You will, I am sure, disapprove of what I have done but I hope that you will at least acknowledge that it was once, a long time ago, important to me.

I want to ask your help to complete my research journey. Please know what I am asking is for good not ill. It is only through you that I can rest peacefully, knowing that what I wanted has been accomplished. This is the last leg.

It is an act of faith, of trust. I am not, nor ever have
been, in a position to demand it. I have not been fair
or truthful with you. All I can do is <u>hope</u> that you
will do what I ask.

Ambrose will organise everything from now but
I hope you understand that for reasons of safety
and security (your own) you cannot know more
at this stage.

Dad.

I refold the letter carefully, slide it back into the
envelope.

He's watching me closely. 'You all right?'

I'm shaking. 'I don't know. I don't know,' is all I
can say.

'Before I let her in, can you come back later?' he
says. 'Tonight? There's more but I can't get it yet.'

'When?' I say.

'After closing time. I'll be here.' He starts to move
towards the door.

'Is it me?' I say, and he stops. 'Is it me they want at
Rees? Because of this? What you told me?'

'They don't know about it. Not yet. Not about what
you're carrying. No one knows but us.' He squeezes
my arm, then lets go. 'I'll let her in now. Remember
your promise.'

I nod but under my skin I'm numb. He's opening
the door. 'Ah, coffee. Grand,' he's saying.

She comes over. 'You OK?' She can see I'm not but
I smile anyway.

'Yeah. Yeah, I'm all right.' She offers me a Styrofoam cup. It's the last thing I want but I take it anyway.

'Ben?' says Ambrose.

'Yeah?'

'You all right?' I nod. I look back at Sophy. She's standing stock still, watching us.

He comes out onto the step to see us off – his skin is greenish and waxy in the daylight. He leans over to me and says, '*Tonight*. I'll be waiting.'

The clock sounds the hour over the clanging of the bell as he closes the door, and the noise of London is all around us again.

The key is in my pocket.

21

We're under the clock on the concourse at Waterloo station, waiting and watching the information boards for news of our train, when Sophy says softly, 'Ben, what is it?'

I feel hot and sick and so totally in my own head, it's a while before I answer. 'Nothing. Just … all this. It's doing my head in.'

'I bet. But it sounds like, if you find what he left, then, well, it's finished isn't it? It'll be over. You can … I don't know … give it to the police and …'

I feel myself sinking. I look at her. 'It won't be over,' I say. 'It'll never be over.'

'What do you mean? Of course it –'

The phone Dick gave me rings in my pocket and I pull it out, glad of the distraction. It's Dick. 'Maurice said you were going to London. You still there?' he says.

'Yeah. Where are you?'

'Driving.'

'Is everything OK?'

'Sure. Listen, I got to tell you something.'

'Go on,' I say. The boards are showing our train now.

'Annie Rivers ...' The phones fizzes and I miss it.

'What? *Dick?*'

He's back. 'Annie Rivers is dead. It was on the news. I remembered the name.'

I repeat what he's said to Sophy and she clamps her hand over her mouth, breathes, '*Shit.*' He's going on: 'I couldn't leave it. It was easy to find the address. I figured ...'

'You went there?'

'I was curious. About what you told me, about what she said to you about being careful. About the syringe. I waited till late and I did a little breaking and entering.'

I'm listening but I'm a million miles away. I'm in his study with my sleeve pushed back, the blue vein raised, watching the blood – my blood – rolling into the tube. '*And?*'

'And. I found something.'

'So what was it? What happened to her?'

'Not about her. But I did find out what she found out, if you follow me.'

Sophy's pulling me towards platform 17, and the air on the phone whispers and crackles, and Dick's voice dips in and out. 'On her laptop. I had to hunt for it; found it in a file marked "Sewing" – get it? Needles?' He waits. We're on the train now. 'I opened it.'

'Dick, for fuck's sake – you're doing my head in. Just *tell* me.'

'OK, OK.' The train driver begins his droning announcements then, about where he's taking us, and I'm straining to hear Dick.

'David Collins: Aconite Hydrochloride.'

'What?'

'Aconite Hydrochloride,' he shouts, 'that was it. That was what was in the syringe.'

'What? What is it?' says Sophy, leaning in. I hold the phone so we can both hear.

'It's a type of … poison,' he's saying.

'Never heard of it. That's what killed him?'

'I guess.'

'So he *was* murdered.'

'Mmm.'

'What do you mean, mmm?'

'Well, it's a plant poison from some kind of South American orchid. It can be deadly of course, just seems like an odd thing to use, that's all.'

'Odd?'

He goes on. 'Ben, what happened exactly after you found your dad? Who did you call? Who was there?'

And then I have to tell him that I don't know. That I called for Charlie and left him to handle it while I ran away and hid like a child.

'So you don't know? You never asked your brother?'

'No.' I do not want this conversation. I lie back against the seat and the movement of the train rumbles up my spine and down again.

'I found something else in her apartment,' he says.

'What?'

'Letters. Love letters, pretty passionate ... and a picture. Tucked away.'

'Who from?'

'A woman, name of Nora Blane. Ring any bells for you?'

'Shit! Nora Blane, the one who –'

'Jumped off the bridge. Correct. She worked at Rees too. Another bio-chemist. Another mysterious ending.'

'Then why didn't Annie *say* something, tell us she suspected them?'

'I guess she was scared, Ben. With good reason. Aren't you?'

Sophy and I look at each other. My head's reeling.

When we get back, I walk Sophy to her place and her mum opens the door. She's smaller than Sophy but with the same red hair and blue eyes. She looks right through me, and I can feel Sophy bracing herself.

'I've been calling and calling,' she says, 'you said you were going to be at Emily's, and, *guess what?*'

'I know. I know. I'm sorry. My phone –'

'Why was your phone switched off? You know I worry. You've just been ignoring me. Have you *any idea* how worried we've been?' She turns to me then and snaps, '*Why are you still here?*'

'*Mum,*' says Sophy.

'And what's happened to your face?' she says, glancing

at me in horror. I can't speak. It's like the words just creep under my tongue and die. I stare at the ground.

'Just get inside,' she says to Sophy.

There's a pause. I step back, and her mum stands aside for Sophy to go in. But she doesn't. Instead, she says, 'No,' and her face is set. 'No. I'm seventeen years old. I do my work, I get good grades, I do everything I'm told, I *never* give you any trouble, and if I want to spend some time with my boyfriend, then you can't stop me.'

And Sophy shoots a look at me and she's biting her lip. In spite of everything, I find I can't not smile. She takes my arm and walks me to the gate, leaving her mum with her mouth open, holding onto the door for support.

When we get to the gate, I can't quite work out the expression on her face.

'Was that … was that OK?' she says, 'what I said? It just came out … I hope …'

I stop her. I take her in my arms and kiss her, and she tastes of mint and salt, and again I feel that jolt through me – like a bloody great Catherine Wheel. Like for a moment, I can block out what Ambrose told me and what he's going to tell me, and how I was used and what I am or might be because of it. With her, it's not complicated. It's good and I want it to last for ever.

But then her mum's right behind us. 'Out,' she says to me, although I am technically on the pavement already. Ignoring her, I whisper in Sophy's ear, 'You're amazing.'

She takes my hand and squeezes it. 'Be careful.' I turn to go and she pulls me back. She says softly, 'I love you.'

I feel incredible for exactly seven minutes. As long as it takes to get home. I'm fiddling with my key in the lock, when Karen opens the door. Like Sophy's mum, she doesn't look happy. Her eyes are red and her cheeks are blotchy, and she stands rigid in the doorway massaging her elbows.

'Where have you been? Your phone's dead, I've been trying to call you.'

I shrug and try to go past her but she blocks my way.

'I was out,' I say. 'Just *out*.'

'Oh, no! You are not going on that bloody Xbox until you've told me what you're up to, where you've been – I found the place in a terrible state this morning. You know I've got better things to do than –'

'Just leave me the fuck alone, Karen!'

I go to walk away again but she gets up in front of me. 'Do NOT talk to me like that! If your dad were here now –'

'He's not here is he? No one is. It's just me.'

She looks at me, all wounded now. 'I do my best, Ben. I look after you, I clear up after –'

'I don't want it! I don't want any of it. You're not my mum. I don't need looking after.'

There's a silence then, one of those deep, horrible, gory quiets that gets right up in your ear canal. And then I think she's going to cry and I'd rather have my toenails pulled out than listen to that. Because if I don't keep it together right now, I could give her a run for her money: I could cry for England. But she doesn't, she looks at me and says more gently, 'What is this all about?'

I swallow, hold it in. 'All I'm trying to do is find out what happened.'

'What do you mean, *what happened*?'

'I think Dad –' hard to say the word. 'I don't think it was suicide, that's all.'

'Sorry. I still don't …'

'I think he was killed. That it was made to look like suicide –'

She cuts in then, and her voice is back on the usual Mary Poppins register. 'You're playing too many of those silly video games. For heaven's sake, it was on the death certificate.'

'Whatever.' I shrug and go to the study but she follows me, and we stand facing each other just inside the room. I hear her swallow and the faint tick of her tongue on the roof of her mouth.

'Look, Ben, I know it's been hard on you but really the best thing you can do is try to get back to normal, get on with your life.'

'Normal? *Normal?* There is no normal. Not anymore. Not for me. You must know that. I mean, you do *know* me, right?'

'You were in shock. It was a terrible shock for all of us –'

'Yeah.'

'He was *my* brother.'

'I know he was your brother. And you know what? You can do what you like. I'm not telling anyone else how to deal with this. I'm just doing what *I* need to do.'

'Yes but –'

'*Are you listening to me?*' I'm squeezing back tears now. 'Like I say, you can do whatever the fuck you like about him: plant a tree, write a song, I don't care. But me, I think – I don't *think, I know* – there's something going on and I need to find out what.'

I step back and fold my arms. I can't tell what she's thinking but she's listening at least. 'Look, when I saw Dad – *there* – I thought it was *my* fault. That I somehow *made* him do it. I was miserable and angry about Mum, about everything I guess and I took it out on him – he hadn't done anything – it wasn't his fault but I just … I punished him, for nothing – for being the way he was and it was mad, because I loved him. I really loved him. But now I know different. Now everything's changed and I have to know it all now, because if I stay like this I'm going to lose it. I know it. And you can't stop me.'

I look hard at her and there are tears in her eyes. She puts out her hand to touch mine but I slide it back under my arm.

'So, who do you –?' she says.

'His work. It's something to do with his work. I can't go into it now but I found out stuff, about Rees, about what they were into, about him. There were others too.'

Behind her, stacked against a wall, I can see the engravings.

'*Others?* What others?'

'At Rees. Around twelve people who worked there died in ... in suspicious circumstances between 2011 and 2013. Made to look like suicides but some people don't think so. Dad was the last.' And then I think of Annie Rivers. 'No that's not true, someone else died. They got to someone else. Someone who was helping me.'

Her face is white and she says, almost to herself, 'He hated that place.'

'*Really?*'

'Really.'

'Why? What did he say about it?'

'Didn't have to say anything. It was written all over his face. You know he never slept?'

It was true. I'd wake in the night sometimes and hear the soft snap of a door, or the ring of a glass.

'Karen, what happened when he died, do you know?'

'I don't know. Charlie dealt with it, bless him. We were away, remember? Charlie called us and we got the first flight we could.'

'What did he say?'

'Just that ... that David had ... you know ... in the car.'

I nod.

'One of your neighbours – I don't know who – went with him in the ambulance. He came back with the death certificate. Charlie just couldn't bear to ...'

'No.'

'Ben love, I am sorry about your dad. I know he was difficult, he found people hard, you know, and he was very preoccupied with his work. It meant so much to him. But he … he did love you – you and Charlie. *And* your mum, she was his *rock*, his *lifeline* to the rest of the world. I know that sounds silly but she was.'

I see her then. It's Visiting Hour. She's pale and bloated and she's lost her hair from the chemo. Charlie's holding her hand, and I'm standing next to her bed and I'm pouring her a glass of water, and the glass isn't glass at all but some weird fluted plastic. There are fine little scratches all over it. I look out of the double doors onto the corridor outside and I see his face against the window. Watching.

I look at the engravings again and something cold threads its way under my skin.

22

She puts out a hand again, and this time I let her take mine. Her fingers are small and thin like the wings of a bird. 'I am sorry, dear.'

I nod and look away. 'Can I …?' I say. 'I need to do some work in here.'

'Yes. I have to go anyway. I made you something but … you're very welcome to come back with me if you want. You're always …'

'I know. Thanks. I'm sorry about what I said. I didn't –'

She looks at me and sniffs. 'It's OK. I know it's … hard.' She turns to go, then looks back. 'You will be careful, won't you?'

I go to the front door and watch her leave. The sky is darkening and the air is thick with static and as I close the door, the first crack of thunder, like a rolling barrel, rips towards me.

The study's clean now. His papers sit in tidy piles on

the desk and the shelves above it. Each pile is weighted with a small glass paperweight.

I catch my reflection in the window. I can't see my eyes – just black sockets in a pale face.

Being in here now after what Ambrose told me, I feel different: dry, empty somehow; and further away from my father than ever.

There are six engravings from the Inferno lying against the wall, all by the same artist. I lay them out on the floor: bleak and angry portraits of human misery and despair; of punishment and humiliation. The second one I come to is the one I want. I stand in silence for a moment, studying the picture in its place in the group. The man in the woods, haunted and alone, looks back at me over his shoulder.

I take the picture and lay it on the desk. I'm studying it when something makes me look up. Pressed against the window, like a white starfish, is a hand. I can't see what's behind it. It lifts and bangs hard on the pane and a face appears. Sophy.

'Jesus, you scared me,' I say as I let her in. She's shivering and her hair hangs down her back like wet weeds. 'I'll get you a towel.'

She nods, too cold to talk, and I rush upstairs, three steps at a time, and hunt out a towel that doesn't smell too bad.

When I'm back I say, 'What happened with your mum?'

'I just said I was going out,' she says. 'I couldn't stay

at home, and they know they can't stop me.'

'They wouldn't dare,' I say, and I take her in my arms but she wriggles free.

'I'm not here for that, I'm here to help.' But she kisses me anyway. 'Is this it?'

We pore over the surface of the print. Nothing out of the ordinary. And then I turn it over. It's set in a narrow gilt frame and, on the back, there's an insert of card with brown tape around the edges to seal it. Sophy runs to the kitchen for a knife.

'Go for it,' she says.

Carefully, I work my way around the paper tape with the knife and soon the card backing falls away. Underneath it, the back of the print is revealed. The paper's soft and porous to touch, and smells faintly of mould. Someone's written on the back in ink that was probably smudged as the card backing was replaced.

A diet of worms. The earth shall render up. Dig.

She looks at me. '*Worms? Dig?*'

'Dig. Something buried?'

'Render. Render means *give up*. We'll find it if we dig for it.'

'OK. The garden?'

We go through the house to the back door, and look out at the garden. It's pretty much all paving stones with a fence at the end. It's neat, suburban. Then it comes to me: 'I know: worms – the diet of worms – they break down waste, they eat waste, make compost. He was obsessed with them, with the whole thing. He had an allotment. There's a massive compost dump there, on his patch. He was always on about it – composting everything – food, waste, rubbish … anything organic. I reckon that's it.'

'OK. So …'

'It's not far.'

We go up the hill and through a small barred gate that leads to an alleyway. The rain is easing as we cross the main road and go along a tree-lined street that curves and weaves and opens at the far end onto the allotments, a rag-tag patchwork of gardens dotted all about with little sheds and lean-tos.

I haven't been there for years and the smell of wet earth and wood smoke creeps up my nose and stays there.

The gates are locked but the fence is broken halfway along.

I know where his patch was – looks like no one's claimed it. It's a large one, about a hundred feet square. Long fingers of grass and weeds bend in the wet wind. The ground is broken up into thick clods of mud and, in the greenhouse, rotting onions loll on their hooks like shrunken heads. The compost site is in the middle of the allotment and I go into his old shed for a pitchfork. It isn't locked. The door swings open on its hinges with a creak. I stand for a minute, breathing in creosote and must, and suddenly the space in the shed fills up with him.

I get out quick and go to where Sophy's waiting by the compost. A dark stew of soil and cuttings seething with worms, it's a crude box bordered on all sides by thick planks of timber coated with a black weatherproofing mix. I climb in.

The fork pierces the mulch, and I twist and turn it to break up the soil. I send Sophy to the shed for a spade and then I go at it. For about ten minutes I dig into the black froth, casting it away from me in all directions, with Sophy making encouraging noises from the sidelines. I'm about to give up when the spade hits something hard. We hear it: the smack of metal on metal.

Sophy climbs in and we both kneel down and use our hands to claw and push the remaining compost away.

It's a large metal trunk with a heavy hasp, about six inches long, secured by a padlock. My father's name is picked out in white paint on the lid. We hoist the trunk out of the compost bin and set it down in the weeds. We look at each other and after a moment, Sophy says, 'What about the key? Have you got it?'

I fumble in my pocket for it. Once in the padlock, it turns with a groan and springs the lock.

The chest is full of bubble wrap. We clear that away and underneath is my father's laptop and under that, a box of papers. Sophy says, 'Let's get it into the shed.'

Once inside, I feel about in the grit and dust for candles and matches and Sophy takes out the laptop and opens it. Tucked inside is a piece of paper titled: 'Welcome to Hell.'

It reads:

My name is David Collins and this is my valediction:

At Rees, I was one of many who spent our working
lives in the pursuit of death and disease. We chased
death: hounded it, moulded it, in test tubes, in crop
sprays, in babies' bottles. We were paid to research
new ways to destroy people: communities, babies
in their mothers' wombs, children. For many years,
I worked tirelessly to master new ways of killing,
all in the name of Science. It was at Rees that I
truly passed through the gates and crossed the river
into Hell. It was there that I witnessed corruption
and greed beyond all measure and this is what I lay
before you now, in the deepest sorrow and shame for
those I have damaged and lost.

The candle I've lit gutters and casts our shadows
high against the walls. Sophy reaches for my hand but
I don't want whatever it is she's offering right now. Not
pity, or love, or a pat on the back. I don't deserve it. I'm
reeling from it all. It's like poison, sudden and bitter,
and on the back of what I know now, plus the letter
he left for me at the bookshop, I'm out. I'm beyond it.
I can't handle it.

She follows me out of the shed, and I stand up to
my ankles in mud, watching my breath blowing in front
of me. 'Ben?' she says softly.

'No. *Don't.*'

She looks hurt. 'I was just going to say … we should
take it back – take all of it back to yours.'

'Yeah,' I say but I'm not really listening.

'*Ben?*'

I say, 'I can't … it's just … this is it. My dad. This is

what I've got – all I've got.'

'But this is what you wanted, to find what he left before Rees …'

I look at her. I want to tell her about him, about what he's done to me, what I'm carrying but I can't. She goes on, 'And this – this isn't all you've got. You've got me.'

I can't answer that the way I want to because it would hurt her and it's not her fault.

I don't remember how we get back. We leave the trunk in the shed and take the contents. And when we're home, I put the box of papers on the floor and the laptop on his desk, plug it in and open it. We wait while it ticks and taps and whirrs into life and the box on the screen asks for a password.

'Acheron?' she says. I nod but I'm sinking again. And not for the first time, I'm asking myself what it was that made me *ever* want to do this – to go this far – and what the hell I'm going to do now.

It works.

There's one file on the desktop marked Rees.

In the pages that follow, there are copies of emails – hundreds of them – and I notice the name Aiden James. In the box, there are photographs and newspaper cuttings relating to the deaths of scientists at Rees; there are classified letters from foreign powers; documents going back years, detailing death rates; carefully annotated photographs of people blighted and disfigured with disease. I see the name Lebeque, the village in France that lost so many to a mystery virus; other places too are listed. And all the official documents carry the stag crest of Rees Global.

My head's throbbing. I stand up. 'I've got to go,' I say, 'back to Red Gull. I said I'd go back there tonight. He said he's got something for me.'

She gets up too. 'I'll come with you.'

'No. No. You're OK.'

'But …'

I look at her and she's shining like she always is, and I think about what kissing her was like and the feel of her against me, and I know that's all I can hope for, for now, all I can hold onto. 'Sophy,' I say, 'you've been so great. I …'

'What?' she says, '*What?*'

'I just can't do this … with you. I'm so … *fuck it*, you're too good for all this – all this bullshit.'

She just stands there watching me and her eyes are burning. '*That's* bullshit. Right there. You don't get to decide what I –'

'Yeah. Actually, I do. When it's about me, about my family.'

'But I want to help you.'

I work my voice back down my throat and I try for gentle but it comes out like spit. 'I don't want *help*. I don't need it. Stop trying to *help* me. I'm sorry, *I'm sorry*. That came out wrong. *Sophy?*'

But yeah, good job, Ben. Classy. She's out the door and I see her walking away, hunched against the cold.

Alone again, just how you like it.

The desk is littered with papers and on the laptop, the screen is black. I close it up and shuffle the papers back into the box. A photograph slips out: a close-up of someone's bare back, a boy about my age I think. I can see the muscle under the skin and his ribs like the staves on a barrel. His skin is covered in dark lumps crusted like scabs. They've used a flash on the camera and there's a glare from the wall behind him. I feel sick.

It occurs to me that right now, I could throw it, all of it. *Burn it.* Wipe the laptop, give it to Rees the next time they come calling and be done with it. No one would know.

Or.

I can do what he wanted. I can use what I've got to end them.

I've buried enough shit.

I call Dick, who comes right over.

'Jeez,' is all he says and he does a lot of whistling through his teeth.

I give him the laptop, the papers, password, everything. 'Dick, I have to go. Can you … take care of it? Give it to the right people? I think that's what he wanted – I think this way I can … *we* can finish them.'

He nods and does a kind of salute, and I think at first he's taking the piss but when I look at him, his eyes are full. 'You're a good man, Ben. I'm proud of you.'

I get to Red Gull at half past five. The sign says CLOSED. I rap on the door and wait. The old book on the velvet cloth is still there in the window and the blind is down on the door.

After waiting a bit, I go to the shop next door, another bookshop called Comics for Collectors, and find the owner, a woman with a purple quiff and tinted glasses. She's just closing up.

She shakes her head. 'Haven't seen him. I know he went out around lunchtime, then I heard him banging around in there this afternoon and it's been closed since. He might be having a nap – can I leave a message for you?'

I shake my head and leave, then I spend a good thirty seconds hammering on the door with my fists. The blind swings at the glass and the bell jangles reproachfully. From far inside, I think I hear a plaintive mewing.

A traffic warden stops and looks in my direction. 'They're closed,' he says helpfully.

'Right.' I nod and stand back. To the side of the shop, in the alleyway, there's a high, blackened brick wall with barbed wire looped along the top. A telephone box stands against the wall, and, checking I'm not being watched, I climb up on top of it. After some grappling and slipping, I find myself crouching on its domed top, looking down a long drop into a weedy, cobbled back yard covered in bird shit.

I take a deep breath and launch myself off the box, clearing the barbed wire, and land feet first in the yard.

There's a back door with a stained-glass panel. I push the handle down and find it unlocked. It leads onto

a little kitchen with tiled floors and an old-fashioned
sink. In the middle of the room is a plastic table with
three glasses on it. All empty. Another door leads off the
kitchen, and I guess this goes into the shop.

I push the door to the shop. It's heavy but there's
more than that: something's blocking it. I hear the scrape
and groan of something bulky resisting. There's a thin
wailing sound too, coming from the other side. I try
again. The whining noise gets worse and I heave at the
door with all my strength to release what's blocking it.
And then in ten seconds flat I wish I hadn't.

23

Half-light. Blinking. The floor near the door is sticky – treacle swill of something underfoot.

Empty shelves: books scattered and upended here and there – their stiff leather backs broken. Scuffs and marks in the dust.

And sitting slumped over the table with his tribal spear stuck through his neck is Ambrose.

I ease around the table, gently rock him back. His eyes bulge from their sockets, his mouth is loose and wide and his clothes are drenched in blood. I feel a rush of salt over my tongue, and choking, I run back to the sink and hurl.

For a long time after, I sit on the floor in the kitchen with my head in my hands, with his cat weaving around me. Laughter licks up from the alleyway, and a police siren moans in the distance. Eventually I stand up, my head spinning, and I force myself to go back into the room.

I look at my watch: it's five minutes to six.

I make myself look at Ambrose again. The tip of the blade shows through the skin of his throat. His jaw is slack, his face badly bruised like he's been beaten, and his tongue spills over his teeth. I look and I look, and there's something not right. There's a kind of lump in his left cheek – a puffiness that stretches the skin.

I walk over.

Up close, his tongue is already discoloured, dark and thick. Again, I feel bile rising in my throat. I swallow it down. I push my fingers into the open mouth. It sucks me in, spongy and dry.

There's something stuffed inside his cheek: a small ball of paper, scrunched very tight with thin strings of blood and saliva clinging to it. I open it out.

One word: *Cuckoo.*

A fly hums about us in the gloom. Cuckoo means mad maybe? A bird? *Another* bookshop? Something else out of Dante? Something to do with my father? I look at the word again. The writing is a scrawl, it lists this way and that, and the last 'O' tails and bleeds away across the page like there was more to say.

My head's empty. I'm spinning further and further away from anything and everything I know.

Just then, there's a whirring and a grinding and the clock at the front of the shop begins to sound the hour. It breaks into the silence and I guess that's why I pay attention.

At the top, through a little opening, a bird pops out six times to give the hour.

'*Cuckoo clock*,' I hear myself whisper.

It's on the wall over the front door and it's massive. It's carved out of wood in the shape of a house with a pitched roof and there are two long chains hanging down from it at different lengths. Around the house are carvings of animals and birds that creep and crawl in and out of the shadows.

Standing on tiptoe I can just reach it. I unhook it and it comes away easily. It's far heavier than I expected though and it rattles like there's something inside it that maybe shouldn't be there. I raise it up and bring it down hard on the ground, and it shatters, sending splinters of wood across the floor.

In among the broken wood and the bits of mechanism, is a small package with the words 'For Ben' on the front. I take a breath and unwrap it. Inside is a British passport, an airline ticket dated tomorrow to Kunming in Yunnan Province, Mainland China, and Chinese money. With it is a handwritten note:

> You were followed. They're on to me. I need to disappear.
>
> Be very careful.
>
> You'll be met at the other end at the airport. Everything will be explained. Good luck. Ambrose.

I'm reeling.

My dad's letter is still in my pocket: 'I want your help to complete my research journey ...' I take it out and read it over and over again, and he comes up at me in every gap between every word. But I still don't understand what he wanted and, more to the point, I don't know how much I'm prepared to give. Is he really asking me to be a part of this warped alter-universe of death and disease? To actively, consciously make an effort to *complete* something he started? Except I already am. I am a part of it. He saw to that.

I open the passport and my face stares out from the back page. But the name doesn't match. It's for a Jack Scott. The address is different too. I walk to the door and lift the blind to see people hurrying past in the street, clutching their coats against the cold. The wind whistles and rattles at the thin glass.

I feel myself rooting into the ground, feel it tugging at me, holding me. I could stay here for ever. I take out my own phone and switch it on. I know what Dick said about them tracking me but I don't care. There's a thousand missed calls from Karen but I press Charlie's number.

It rings for ages and then he picks up.

'Hey.' His voice sounds distant.

'Hey.'

'Are you OK? What's going on? Karen called. Where were you?'

'I'll tell you later. How are you?'

'You got laid, didn't you?'

I'm folding. Hearing his voice, knowing he doesn't know, can't know, what I am … my voice breaks.

'Shut up,' I say. He thinks I'm joking. He laughs, a

throaty wheeze that gets to me I don't even know how.

'Well. How are you? What's up?' he says.

How do you answer a question like that when there's a dead man behind you? 'I'm OK,' I say, and again: 'I … how are you?'

'Yeah. All right. Knackered. Crucified's more like it. Tell me why I did this again?'

I go through the motions: 'I have no idea. Because you're a trigger-happy wanker?'

'Thanks mate. So come on. What's up?'

I don't know where to start. 'It's about Dad.'

'Dad what?'

I want to tell him everything but I don't let myself. I say, 'I … found a letter from him.'

'You *what*?'

'I think he was in trouble before he died – something to do with what he was working on. I think … at least I *don't* think it was suicide.'

I hear him whistle under his breath. Then, calm and quiet: 'Go on.'

'Rees have been on my case. They keep saying he stole something from them.'

'What, Dad? *Steal* something? That's bullshit.'

'No, no. He did take stuff. He took loads of stuff – secret stuff – classified – about what they were doing – weaponising germs – testing them. I think he was in it up to his neck. Did you know?'

He doesn't answer straightaway. I can hear him walking. Then he says, 'I wondered. I'd read about Rees

– websites and shit. I asked him about it once – he'd never talk about it though.'

'Anything else?' I say.

'Anything else what? What do you mean?'

'Like … I don't know, at home. Did you know about anything he was doing, planning?'

There's a silence. 'No. No, mate, I don't know what you mean.'

He's telling the truth. I know he's telling the truth.

I say, 'Along with the letter and everything else …'

'Yeah?'

'He sent me a ticket to China.'

'You're kidding. *China?*'

'I know. Do you think—?'

'What? Do I think *what*?'

'I don't know. The letter says he wants me to go to China to … *complete* his research or something.'

There's a pause. And then he says, 'No. No. You're asking me what I think? Don't go. Tear up the letter. Burn it and walk away and get on with your life. Whatever toxic scheme this is, you do *not* want to get mixed up in it. Listen. What's there for you in it? I'll tell you: nothing. Leave it mate. I tell you. Leave it alone. It's full of shit.'

'But it's Dad. It's from Dad. I mean whatever he did, he must have …' and I tail off in a whiney dribble.

'Ben, you're insane. Maybe we all are. Look, just forget about it. Do not do this, OK? You hear me? Don't do anything. Ben, I can't come home now – there's all sorts of shit going on here – you wouldn't believe – seriously fucked up stuff coming at us – all of us – I never thought I'd … never mind, I've got some leave coming. Just hold the line yeah? We'll have a beer.' He waits. 'It's good to hear from you, I mean it.'

'Yeah. You too. Take care. And thanks.'

'*I mean it*.' There's a sharp click and he's gone. And I know, in spite of what Charlie said, I have to do this, I can't ignore it. It won't let me.

I unbolt the front door and go quickly down Charing Cross Road towards Trafalgar Square. I dive into a phone box and call 999, tell them about the body in the Red Gull bookshop and hang up stat when they ask me my name. There's bile in my throat and I can't stop my teeth from grinding. I keep my eyes on my feet and watch the pavement under me. Words and images tangle in my head: *midway on life's journey; the path through the woods; I did not die and I did not remain alive; abandon all hope* … my father paying the ferryman to cross the river into Hell; Charlie; and now China? And over it all, hovers the twisted form of Ambrose Bellamy with a spear through his neck in that dusty room.

Maybe this is like Dante, maybe I need to go on this journey through the dark to be able to come out into the light again. As the letter said, this is the last leg. Maybe whatever's waiting for me in China will mean I can get rid of what he did to me, what he did to my blood.

I go to the grey, stone steps of the National Gallery

and lean on the balustrade and watch the tourists
moving among the pigeons. The little package is hot
in my hand.

I have to see Sophy.

24

The journey back goes quickly – I sleep most of the way and wake up just before my stop. I go home, shower, and grab a few changes of clothes, a toothbrush, my phone charger and throw them into a bag with the package. As an afterthought, I write a note for Karen and leave it on the kitchen table: *I'm going away for a few days. I'm all right. Don't worry. See you soon. Ben.*

Feeling a bit more human, I go to Sophy's house.

Her dad's car is gone and the house looks pretty quiet. I ring the bell and wait. And wait. I'm on the point of leaving when I hear Sophy's voice calling, 'Hold on!'

She opens the door. She's in her robe again and her hair is wet. There's a tang of scented steam in the house and the gurgle of bathwater hurrying into the plughole.

I stand there. I don't deserve any of this and I as good as blew it last time and … it occurs to me maybe I should actually be saying this out loud, not just thinking it.

Her eyes narrow. 'What do you want?'

I take a breath. 'Um. OK. First, to say what an idiot I was, that I'm sorry and so ... so embarrassed about who he – who I am, what he did ... how I don't even deserve to even *think* about you being with me, let alone actually ... you know ... anyway, I –'

I kind of shunt into a verbal siding and grind to a halt. She folds her arms across her chest and her robe tightens and I can see the curve of her breasts under it. I look up quickly.

She says, 'You just pushed me away. You really hurt me.'

'I know. I know,' I say miserably.

'I only wanted to –'

'Don't say it. *Please.* Because that's it. I don't want you to *help me.* Do you understand? I want to ... I want to ... help *you* sometimes. I want *us* to ... Christ.'

'Us,' she says.

'Yes. *Us.*'

There's a long, long silence and I look at her bare feet and their red toenails and my feet in their dirty trainers and I haven't touched her yet although I want to but I can't do anything because I need her to say something – do something. I'm waiting.

She turns away and goes to the stairs, and I stay fixed to the threshold until she looks back and says, 'Are you coming?'

I swallow and close the door and follow her to her room and I'm feeling the weight of what I've said and what's happened like stones. She looks at me, smiles shyly and goes to her dressing table for something. I take one step towards her and then I go and sit down at the end of the bed.

'Where are your mum and dad?' I say.

She's brushing her hair and it shines red-gold down her back. It hurts to not be touching her. 'School thing for Lily – my sister. She's playing the cello.'

I'm not listening. 'Yeah?'

'How was the Red Gull? Did you get whatever it was?'

The last thing I want in the room with me is Ambrose Bellamy's corpse. I nod and having to talk about it is like turning a tanker. I tell her about the letter and the ticket but not about him. She comes over, her eyes round, and sits on the bed.

'Jesus, Ben, *China*? What's that all about?'

'I've got no idea. But … he wanted me to go. There has to be something, or someone there that's connected to all this somehow.'

'So you're going away.' Something in her tone's changing, shifting, slipping.

'I have to.'

'*Have* to?' she says sharply.

'I have to go. I can't tell you why right now because I don't even know myself but I have to see it through.'

'See what through?'

'I don't even know really … I … Sophy, please …'

'OK. Whatever.'

'I should go. You want me to –' I get up slowly and turn to see tears on her face. I go to her then and kneel at the side of the bed. 'Sophy, there's so much in my head right now I just can't talk about it – not to anyone.'

I stroke her hair and she sniffs, and just when I think I'll lean in and kiss her, she says, 'It's just … I don't want you to go. I don't want you to go away. I'll miss you. I'm afraid for you. I …'

I kiss her face. 'Sophy, I'm not going for ever. It's a return ticket. I'll be back before you know. I just need to do this. You understand that, don't you? I'll be back, I promise.'

'You don't know that. It could be a trap. It could be those guys again. *Please*, Ben.'

I climb onto the bed and very slowly I lie back and she puts her head on my chest. I hold her and I lie through my teeth.

'Look. Look what we've been through. I'm a survivor. I know I'm going to be fine. It's just the … the last chapter. It's Dad's writing. His instructions. He set it all up before he died. It's good, it's going to be fine. I know it, it'll be a way to really finish Rees for good, that's what it'll be … and by the way … in case you were wondering … I love you too.'

She looks up at me and I kiss her then and her mouth is so soft under mine. I put my hand under her robe, where her back is smooth and warm. She stiffens for a moment, then I feel her relax. There's the hum of a washing machine from way downstairs but otherwise the house is quiet. The feel of her skin under my hand is electric and suddenly nothing else matters. Her breath comes in sharp gasps. I put my lips against her neck and I breathe her in.

'Ben … I …'

I pull back. 'Am I … are you OK? Is this −?'

'This? I want this …' she says.

'You sure you're OK?'

She sits up, and smiling, she pushes me gently back onto the bed, and she's watching me and I'm watching her, and she pulls at my T-shirt. I let her take it off and every muscle is straining and I can't speak because my heart's going like I've never known, and I don't know what to do and I know exactly what to do. She fits me. She makes me feel all the things I never knew I could feel. Stuff I never knew was in me. That I want to watch over her, to protect her, to be the best I can be for her.

Under her robe, she's wearing a white lace bra and knickers.

I kiss her again and draw her gently back towards the bed. I rock her down so she's sitting astride me. She reaches up and sweeps her hair off her face. I see her long limbs and the arch of her body, and I draw her to me and kiss her, and she catches her breath as I run my fingers up her back. I feel for, and undo the catch on her bra and let it fall. I cup her breasts in my hands and stroke her down the length of her body to the waistband of her knickers. I want her so badly I can hardly breathe. I'm burning. She brushes her fingers down my rib cage to the waistband of my jeans and it actually makes me gasp. We take off what's left of our clothes. Back on the bed, we're skin to skin again and the feeling runs through me like 200 volts.

She leans in and kisses my neck.

'Sophy, that man …' I say, 'what he did to you … I feel so bad – I'll never stop feeling like I caused it … I'm so sorry.'

'Ben.'

'What?'

'Shut up. Kiss me.'

And I do.

Afterwards, I just want to touch her. I can't get enough of her. I want to stay with her forever: the smell of her, the feel of her fingers laced in mine, her soft skin under the sheets as she curves into me and I hook my body around hers. Am I happy? I think right now, in her bed, with her dad probably about to burst in any minute, with me leaving, just now, in spite of everything else, I'm happier than I thought I ever could be or will be again. She takes a picture of my face on her phone: 'To remember you … to remember this.'

And then I know I have to go. I roll out of her bed and gather up my things. I hold her one last time and she breathes into my ear, 'Be careful.'

25

I manage to make it out of the house without being seen, and leg it back to mine. And all the way there, and forever, there's the smell of her, the feel of her, in my heart and in my head.

Later on, I walk to Maurice's. I'm wearing a hat of Charlie's with fur flaps, and I've turned my collar up. It's late when I get there and I bang on the door of the flat.

'Maurice! It's me.'

'All right, all right, I'm coming.'

Maurice is wearing his pants, grey Y-fronts. 'Hello, my friend! How's things?'

I tell him about the ticket, about the passport and the letter but nothing else – I guess by now I don't need to be persuaded how dangerous this is but if anyone did need ammunition to do that, then Ambrose being killed with his own spear would certainly do the trick.

'Cripes,' he says, 'you sure this is a good plan? World's going mad at the moment. Best to stay inside and wait it out – whatever it is …'

He's waiting for me to ask him what he's on about but I can't get it together to care. I say, 'Can you take me to the airport tomorrow?'

He nods. 'If you're sure, old pal,' he says.

I sit on his sofa next to the Alsatian, and watch the eerie avatars hover in and out on the flickering screen. The Alsatian proves surprisingly comfortable and the next thing I know Maurice is shaking me awake. Shafts of sun poke through into the dim room. My phone's still on and I have a text sent late last night from Charlie: *Call me.*

But I don't.

I wave Maurice off at the airport, and he makes the thumbs-up sign as he drives off in a cloud of exhaust.

There's a tetchy queue to get into the terminal – anxious faces, heads turning and craning, and there's armed police in riot gear going up and down the line. No one says anything.

When I get to the doors, there's only one entrance open and a woman in uniform with tired eyes hands me a leaflet and a paper mask from a giant bin. 'Flu epidemic,' she says. 'Nasty one. Please wear this in the terminal and on the plane.'

'Flu?' I say, 'what kind of –'

She stares at me. Someone tut-tuts behind me. 'Just flu,' she says. 'It's a precaution. Please don't make a fuss. Just put it on or someone will make you put it on.' Behind her are two police officers, arms folded across their guns.

Inside, there are more police. Some shops are closed or closing and people are standing by the walls in small groups. Everyone is wearing a mask.

The leaflet is from the World Health Organisation. It says, 'Fears of a pandemic have been greatly exaggerated but it is sensible to take precautions in public places. Wash your hands regularly, use the anti-bacterial hand wipes provided, and please wear your mask in public to avoid contamination.'

I buy a newspaper. I never buy newspapers but something makes me want to.

The front page has reports on a new kind of virus they're calling the new *Black Death*, that's hit Europe, of death tolls rising in western cities, and of scientists racing to find a cure.

Inside, it's the same: pictures, reports, speculation.

And on page 15, a short article entitled: PHARMA GIANT IN GERM WARFARE SCANDAL and, underneath:

> The Bio-Tech arm of multi-national pharmaceutical company, Rees Global, is today under investigation by the authorities after former employee Dr David Collins, who was found dead at his home in May, left a number of documents alleging Rees' involvement in the unlawful development of proscribed bio-chemical substances. The Guardian and the New York Times have obtained detailed information that puts Rees Global at the heart of a black market in germ warfare of the most deadly variety...

There's a photograph of Greenhalgh. He's standing to one side of the picture with his arms folded, looking out at the world with a confident smirk on his face.

My breath in the mask is hot.

I get my phone out and I write a text to Sophy but then I don't send it.

The flight's showing on the boards now. Soon they'll be listing a departure gate. I *could* go home. I could leave now. Get on a train and be home in an hour or two. But I know I'm not going to. Something's making me go through with it. It's like I'm in some kind of track and I can't move out of it. It's too deep. I have to go on.

I go through the gate and take my seat on the plane. I strap myself in, pull the in-flight magazine out of the rack in front of me and look at the Duty-Free ads until the Captain's voice comes over the tannoy and we start taxiing up the runway.

The flight to Kunming is twelve hours long and I stay awake eating peanuts, drinking beer and watching film after film till I can't see straight.

All the crew are wearing masks.

We get into Kunming terminal at 6am. It's massive: glass, with steel struts overhead, and stuffed full of expensive shops.

My head hurts – my hands too – and my mouth is dry as I trudge towards passport control with the rest of the passengers and wait my turn. Fear and lack of sleep are making me edgy, and I need a cigarette.

In the arrivals hall, we're asked to lower our masks

for passport control. A man stands apart from the knot of people meeting passengers, and, I don't know how, but I know straight away that he's waiting for me. He fixes me with a hard, unblinking stare and I stop. He inclines his head slightly and abruptly turns on his heel and walks and I follow, several paces behind. He turns out of the main hall along a walkway that narrows at the end. We go up a flight of stairs to a door at the top. He opens the door onto a small room and stands back for me to go through. There's a plastic table with a chair set either side of it. He offers me a chair and I sit. He remains standing, his hand on the door handle, and in the corner of his right eye a barely perceptible twitch sets up.

'Wait here,' he says.

The door closes and the room is quiet. I swallow air. *What the hell am I doing here?*

I sit, braced, listening to my pulse ticking in my head.

Then out of nowhere I hear footsteps: a flat, heavy tread that comes to a halt outside the door. The sound then of the handle being turned, the metal biting in the groove.

I stand up.

On the threshold is a man. He takes one step forward and says softly, 'Ben.'

My throat burns and my stomach knots. There, in this little room a million miles from home, looking at me with a half-smile, is my father.

26

He's so thin. His clothes hang off him and his face is gaunt. He takes a step towards me and I back away into the room, my mouth open.

He says, 'Is it OK if I sit down?'

He crosses to a chair and as he walks, his hip locks and unlocks with a crunching sound. Sitting, his knees dig like hooks through his trousers. I watch him. He's left the door open and somewhere in a nearby room, there's the sound of a radio: canned laughter and fast Mandarin.

He coughs, and it seems to come from deep inside him and it racks his frame, forcing him to lean back on the chair. I notice his nails are bitten down. He says in a gravelly whisper, 'Did you have a good flight?'

I say nothing.

'I saw you arrive.' He looks around awkwardly. 'I expect this is all a bit of a shock. Would you like a glass of water?'

I shake my head, still staring at him. His eyes are pale, the pupils, pinholes. He puts his hands on the table and knots his long fingers together. A thin smile crosses his pinched face and is gone.

'I'm sorry, Ben.'

He pauses and I know he's waiting for a reaction. I only realise I'm gripping the back of the chair when I feel it start to crack in my hand. I take my hand away and my palm's white with the pressure and sticky with tiny points of blood.

'Ben?'

I shake my head violently, go to leave the room but as I try to pass him he stands up and holds out his hand and it touches mine, and the feel of it – of him – hits me like a whip. I turn to him and our eyes meet, and I fall against him and push my head into his chest. I can smell the sour tang of stale sweat and, underneath it, something very faint that smells of him alone. He takes my shoulders, holds me at arm's length. He's looking at the wall behind me like he always did but there's warmth in his fingers.

'My boy.' And then he drops his arms and starts to cough, holding his fist against his mouth. I'm numb. A dead bird. A bone. A fossil.

He says, 'Sit down.'

I do nothing. Say nothing. '*Please*. Sit down. We haven't got very long. I know you'll want some sort of …' he coughs again, '… explanation.'

I lower myself into the chair and wait. He sits too

and leans forward. 'I expect you know by now a little of what I was involved in at Rees. My work.'

He gets up again, paces to the wall, and says to himself more than to me: 'Where to begin?' He sighs, then rips into it fast.

'I know you might find it hard to understand but I've always been fascinated by disease: its strategies, its campaigns, how it works on the body. The infinite … adaptability … the sheer *intelligence* of it. I developed an enormous respect for illness and infection – the power it could have. I suppose some quack psychologist would say I wanted some of that power for myself: to own, to understand it at least. And at Rees I got that. They gave me the space, the opportunity to fly: to create without boundaries.'

Again I say nothing. I swallow hard to loosen my throat. He takes a breath and continues, still at the same mad speed. 'I climbed the ladder pretty quickly there. All they asked was that you were able to … to think the unthinkable. And, well, some people couldn't handle it. People I'd worked with for years. There was no place at Rees for people who weren't committed, you see, absolutely focused – it was a baseline expectation there and, of course, once you'd worked in the department, once you'd seen and heard … well, leaving – checking out – was impossible – it was very sensitive.'

He stops and moistens his lips.

'They killed people. *You* killed people,' I say.

He sits back down at the table, facing me. 'Yes.'

There's a tremor in his voice, a kind of high-pitched whine behind the words. My head starts to pound again.

He reaches out a hand but then curls it back. 'Ben, I don't find it easy to … show my feelings the way some people do but, if I could – if I did – I would *show* you how wrong I've been, how disgusted I am with what I've done and how terribly, terribly sorry I am.'

I run my hands into my hair and leave them there. I can't look at him. 'You *used* me – my body – my *blood* – you fucking poisoned me and you never told me, asked me … you just –' I can't find the words.

'Ambrose told you then,' he says.

I sit back. 'Just tell me what you're doing here and what I'm doing here and let me go.'

He stifles a cough. 'To do that, I have to go back a long way. From the moment I got interested in the subject, long before I started at Rees, I wondered how possible it would be to create an intelligent, adaptive virus from scratch: something entirely, utterly resistant to heat, to radiation – something that could be both water and air-borne – something that would effectively close down the immune system of the host. It was all on paper, you understand, but I knew it would work: the ultimate virus; something completely new. I'd been looking at parasitic fungi in insects and what they do to the host: they drive them mad, you see, completely take over the brain and the body and use them as a kind of launch pad for an explosion of spores. They can wipe out a whole colony. One ant, once infected by the fungus parasite, can release thousands of spores – incredible. So you see,' he goes on, like he's talking to himself, 'I thought – and I think I was the first to do so – *why not create a hybrid*? A virus *within* a fungus carrier, something that would work like that only in a human host.'

He's shaking. It's like I'm watching him on film – like I'm not even in the room anymore but a thousand miles away.

He goes on. 'I want you to understand it started as a purely scientific endeavour. It was only at Rees when … well –'

'At Rees?'

'They took an interest.'

'And?'

'At Rees I was working on ways of weaponising germs: anthrax, yellow fever and so on – in the abstract, in a lab, to see what *could* be done, not, of course, whether it *should* be. It wasn't legal of course: they were selling these diseases on the international black market, under the radar. One day I told a senior colleague about what I was working on and they wanted to see it.'

'So you let them?'

'I wanted to see it made. I know what you think, Ben, and I know why, but it was a scientific pursuit – a sort of *game* – it's hard to explain to someone who –'

'Who has a problem with killing people?' I snap.

He nods. 'I accept that. At Rees they gave me the space and the funds to develop it, to actually *make* it.' His eyes glitter. 'Once it's aerosolised – used – it tells your cells to host the fungus. I mean you get them to work together. It's never really been done in this way before.' He looks at me anxiously. 'Ben, can you see something of what I mean? Something of the ... I was on the verge of something big. It was so pure ... so *seductive*. It was going to change the way wars were fought.'

He breaks off and leans forward on his elbows. 'The excitement of getting so close. The challenge. The sheer headiness of –'

I get up and walk to the door. Without looking at him, I say, 'Did Mum ever know? About what you were doing?'

He's quiet for a minute, then he locks his bony hands together over his chest. 'No, she didn't. Not about that. I couldn't tell anyone.'

He coughs into his fist again and a lacework of spittle stays suspended between fist and chin until he wipes it away. 'Rees were very excited. They were pushing me to work on it – all day and every day – to finish it, weaponise it – they had buyers in the line. People were taken off other projects to work on it under me and then ...'

'What? *Then* what?'

He sucks in a mouthful of air and his eyes fill, and he says, 'Then ... everything changed.'

'I don't –'

'Something happened that stopped me dead in my tracks and made me question everything I'd ever done, everything I'd been about. It took me out of the lab, made me see the base, loathsome creature I'd become, the terrible, *Faustian* pact I'd made.'

His eyes are wet and he pushes at them with the heels of his hands. 'She got sick.'

'Mum?'

'I remember her face. I remember her face, Ben. Whatever it did inside her, it took her face away. She was so … *beautiful*,' he stumbles on the word like he's never heard it before, '… and it picked her apart. And the worst of it was I understood it. I knew everything about the disease, its pathology, its trajectory, how it reproduces itself, how it *uses* its host … And all I could do was watch it. That was all I could do … because I'd devoted my life to making diseases like it.'

'Jesus,' I breathe.

'I pushed on with the project. I tried to separate what I was doing from what was happening to her. I had to force myself to go into the lab. It got harder and harder to rationalise, to … justify. And she was getting worse. And there came a time, in the last year of her life when I couldn't go on. I told Rees I was mothballing the project and I helped set up a programme for cancer treatment – gene therapy – you were a part of that, as you know – before … before I … I wanted to cure rather than destroy. I was just senior enough to make the transition. Or so I thought. They made life difficult for me over the years but they told me they'd gone along with it and shelved the project.'

'OK. And?' I say.

'It was only much later I learned they'd never closed it down, they'd gone on behind my back, recruited a new team to work on it without me.'

'How did you find out?'

'About a year after Mum died, I had a chance meeting with someone, an old colleague, who mentioned it in passing. I was furious. I went to the CEO, argued with him, said it was my intellectual property and I wanted it destroyed. He was implacable. He said it was made at Rees and it belonged to Rees and they were going ahead with it.'

'So they made it? They finished it anyway?'

'Sort of. Yes.'

'*Sort of?*'

'Up to a point. Which is where I needed you again.'

'I thought I was helping you – after Mum died, I thought you were carrying on with the cancer treatments …'

He pauses. 'I know, Ben. I know. I want to … I … thank you for coming. After all you knew, thank you for trusting me.'

I stare at him. 'I don't believe this,' I say. 'You know Rees have been after *me*? They were looking for what you left – your papers, your –'

'All that – yes. They thought that was it, and in one way, it was. But if they knew the real truth of it, you would have been the far bigger prize.'

'They got to Ambrose.'

'*What?*'

'He's dead. He could have told them what he told me.'

'No.'

'What? Why "no"?'

'Ambrose is very well trained. He would never break.'

I say quietly, 'I thought it was them who killed you.
I thought you'd been murdered like the rest of them.'

'The rest?'

'All those *unexplained* deaths. At Rees.'

'Ah. Of course. But you see that's why I did what
I did. I couldn't bear it any more. I wanted out. More
than that, I … but I knew they'd never let me leave.
With what I knew, what I'd been working on, they'd
never *ever* let me leave. They were close to finishing
the project. I threatened to go to the police, to blow
the whole thing up but they were clever. They … they
said if I tried anything, they'd come for …' his voice
cracks, 'they'd *hurt* you and Charlie.'

'*What?*'

'It was bad, Ben. Those years … I was trapped. And
all the while I knew they were moving ahead with
the project – testing it on live subjects – I couldn't
do anything to stop it because I knew they'd follow
through on their threats. They always do. They were
going to kill me anyway – I knew that – they just
needed me alive a little longer. There were things about
the virus they didn't understand.'

'Go on.'

'It was my only option. Ambrose helped me. I
planned it all carefully. It had to look like suicide. Like

I'd had enough. It was the only way I could be certain they wouldn't touch you and Charlie.'

'You were wrong about that.'

'Possibly but ... I needed to do two things: to bring down the company, and to carry on with what I was doing in secret. I had no option. I won't bore you with too much detail – but I injected a shot of something which can be fatal but in smaller doses can give the appearance of death – slows the heart rate, no pulse, that kind of thing. It would have been almost impossible, you know, to tell – unless you were medically trained. The car's engine was running but the exhaust was attached to a pipe going outside the garage. There was never any carbon monoxide in the car, you see. I had to look dead, feel dead. Ambrose played his part well. It was all arranged. He was with me in the ambulance – which wasn't an ambulance at all. He got the death certificate, made arrangements for a ... a body to be ... er ... cremated.'

'A *body*?'

'A body. Any body. Contact in the morgue,' he says bluntly. 'Not hard to do.'

'Your funeral ... everything. I can't –'

He pauses and his eyelids flicker and twitch. 'I know. Ben, I'm –'

'I ... you *left* us,' I say.

'Ben, I know. I know. But I had no choice. Things had become impossible, *untenable*, more than that: potentially incredibly, savagely dangerous.'

I watch my fingers span against the table top, the veins raised and blue under the strip lights. I take a breath. 'So why did you bring me here?'

He looks down and his eyes are watering. Whether from the coughing or from tears, I don't know. I kick my feet on the carpet. I need a cigarette.

'I don't know how much Ambrose told you but this virus has no cure. There is no vaccine as yet. You come into contact with it, you breathe it in – you die. As I said, it destroys you from the inside out, takes you over. It grows inside you and when it's ready, it pushes itself out of you and explodes. A matter of days and, if the host isn't contained, thousands more will be infected.'

'So, if –' I say.

'I was naive. Of course Rees doesn't bankroll this work as an intellectual exercise. It makes this stuff to sell. This is a virus that's designed to wipe out a population.'

'Like a deterrent, you mean?'

'Possibly.'

'Or …?'

'Or, it will be *used*. Let loose on the New York subway or the London Underground. It's a weapon of war, Ben, just as lethal as a nuclear warhead.'

'*Jesus Christ.*'

'I'm trying to put this right. But I can't do that without you.'

'My blood …'

He's looking at the wall behind me as he says, 'You see, you *are* the virus and you are the *cure*. Only in your body – in your blood – are all the antibodies to destroy it. You're a living prototype – the only one in the world – I know this because I made you.'

I swallow tears. 'You're a monster, you know that?' I say. 'I trusted you. I was a child, for fuck's sake. I was twelve. You were supposed to take care of me – you *promised* her – I know you did. And I'm damaged goods – my blood's *bad* – you did that.'

He covers his face with his hands. 'I know, I know,' he says softly, then after a moment he seems to recover. 'Just hear me out, Ben. I had to go on. Once I found out they were still working on it – on *my virus* – I knew what I had to do. I had to create a vaccine in secret. I needed a living host for the virus that would survive it. A sort of *control*. I began to expose you to the virus in very small, controlled doses so your body would recognise it and make antibodies.'

He puts out his hand to me. '*Please*, Ben. I *had* to do this. I had no option. And it had to be done in total secrecy.'

'Why not Charlie?'

He blinks. 'You were better, more … receptive.' A pause. 'I need you Ben, I need you to help me finish this.'

White bubbles of saliva collect around his mouth. He flashes a glance at me and swallows. His Adam's apple rolls in his neck.

'And if I say no, what? The world's going to end? The sky's going to fall in?'

He looks at me. 'Possibly, yes.'

27

'Are you ready then?' he says.

'For what?'

'We're going into the mountains – to the – to my – village. I want to show you what I've been doing.' He blinks twice and bares his teeth in a kind of grin.

'I don't –' I begin.

'Ben, you came, you trusted me. I won't let you down. I lost the path through the woods and you can help me find it again. We can do this together.'

He goes to the door and turns to me. 'The car's waiting, we need to move.'

'I want to call Charlie.'

'Give me your phone.'

'What? Why?'

He holds out his hand. 'Please?'

I pass it to him and he opens it up, hooks out the Sim and snaps it in half.

'No phones. No contact.'

'What?'

He looks at me hard, shakes his head. 'Surely you understand, Ben? After all I've told you?'

'What the −?'

He sighs. 'As long as you're here, you must stay hidden. Apart from the fact that they can trace you from it, you contact someone in the UK, you tell them where you are, you tell them you're OK, you tell them I'm here − all of that. How soon do you think we'd have visitors here? I have worked *very* hard at this, at staying out of sight. One call, one *text* would damage everything for us.' He eyes me carefully. Sweat stands out on his forehead. 'I'm sorry but that's the way it has to be. And the passport I sent, the money? I'm going to need to take those, too. We can't take any risks.'

I swallow, nod and shove my hand in my pocket, take out the passport and money and give them to him.

'I do hope you can understand, Ben.'

I want to say I'm not coming. But something stops me. He's standing in front of me, wringing his hands together so hard the knuckles shine.

I pick up my bag. 'OK.'

'Thank you.' He smiles at the wall behind me and pats my shoulder but his hand stays stiff. We leave the room and set off down the corridor together.

The car's waiting outside the terminal: a black jeep with a driver. My father holds the door for me, and I slide in across the seat to make room for him but he closes the door and sits in the front seat. We leave at speed, bombing through a cloud of noise and colour, and turn onto a motorway.

I lean forward to the front. 'How far is it?' He doesn't answer, just looks straight ahead. His hands rest in his lap, palms upwards. I repeat, 'How far is it?'

'Oh. About three hours or so. Not long.'

'And I can get back to Kunming tonight?'

He says something to the driver. I don't catch it. Then he turns around. 'Er … not tonight. We're rather off the beaten track where we're going. Rain can knock out the roads if it's bad.'

'So tomorrow then? I can get back tomorrow?'

'Why don't you just enjoy the journey?'

I fall back against the soft leather seats and close my eyes. The car rolls and hums underneath me, and I loll against the window and fade out.

A growling and squealing of gears and brakes wakes me up. We've left the motorway and the ranks of skyscrapers of Kunming and we're on a rough track that winds up steeply through dense forest. Somewhere I can hear fast water on rock, and when I open the window, a thick stew of hot vegetable air hits me. The gears shriek, I'm thrown back in my seat and we're moving fast again, thrusting and lurching upwards into the clouds.

At the brow of the hill, my father asks the driver to stop. He motions to me to get out, and we stand together and look down onto a thickly wooded valley. We're on a ridge that runs away towards mountains, their high peaks clouded in mist. I can hear water rushing, the noise of insects and from far below us, snatches of what sound like voices carried upwards. Rings of sweat are soaking into my shirt and my face burns.

I glance at my father. 'Is that it? Down there? Your village?'

He seems distracted, his body tense and rigid. He extends his arms, spreads his palms out before him, then lattices his fingers together.

He turns to me. 'Ben. There's something else I have to tell you.'

'What?'

'The village. It's not exactly a village. Well. Not in the way you would understand it.'

'What do you mean?'

'It ... it functions as a community. They're pretty much self- sufficient.'

'And? What?'

The driver gets out, leans against the car and lights up. I need a smoke.

'It's just that the ... er ... occupants are not there of their own volition.'

'Eh?'

'It's a prison: a prison camp.'

'A *prison camp*? I don't understand. You said –'

He says, sharply now, 'Ben, I don't think ... I don't think – in spite of what I've told you – that you've quite grasped the severity of the situation. I thought I'd been quite explicit but I don't always express myself ... find the right words. Maybe ...' and he tails off.

I wrap my arms tightly across my body and stare at him, and his eyes flicker up at me and away. He speaks slowly, forcing the words. 'I need you to understand, Rees have the virus – it's out there. What they don't have yet is the vaccine. Only I have that. In you – in your blood. That's what they really want – what they're looking for. But they'll get there on their own in due course. And soon, *very* soon, the virus will be sold, if it hasn't been already. What I started and what they're finishing, will be sold. And no, it won't be kept in pressurised containers in a vault, by a democratic and responsible government. That's not the way Rees do things. It will be sold to people who want to *use* it. On other people. *Yes?* This is not fiction, it's not Hollywood: it's *real*. And it could have the most devastating, shattering effect on a considerable percentage of the world's population. Do you see now why I am anxious to get started? And do you see that, as long as I can do my work, I don't care *where* I do it? I would work on this on the surface of the moon if it meant I could work in secret. Ben, do you see?'

I nod slowly.

'I needed to stay out of sight and I needed protection – security. That's why I'm here. I've been able to set up a small lab here. I pay a little to local officials who look the other way. They don't ask questions and they don't interfere, and I do the same for them.'

At that, he turns and walks to the car, opens my door, pauses a moment, his hand on the handle, and the driver watches us.

'So Rees don't have this? The vaccine?' I say.

He steps back and the leaf litter crackles under his feet. 'People will pay a lot for a weaponised virus; but they'll pay even more for the vaccine. That's why Rees want it. They've tried countless times to get it right but it's eluded them. They'll get there but I want to get there first because once they have it, they'll sell that too and I can assure you, it won't be in a good cause.'

I go to the car and he stands to one side to let me in.

We zigzag downwards, scattering scree before us. The gears whine and grate, and the driver curses. My father is sitting next to me now, his hands lying loosely on his lap. The path narrows at one point, and leaves like spread hands, graze the windscreen. It widens after that and becomes a road. We drive alongside a broad green river that curves and twists under dipping branches to a waterfall some way off. I see two figures: an old man and a boy, both steadying a bicycle laden with timber. They stare as we pass, and the old man waves and smiles with toothless gums.

Suddenly, my father leans forward and grips the back of the driver's seat and whispers something to the driver. Then he sits back and, without looking at me, says, 'We're here.'

Up ahead, are two high gates: iron frames strung with barbed wire. Above them, hangs a small sign printed in red: *Laogai*. Behind them, a guard shouldering a rifle, paces up and down. I look at my father. His face runs with a milky sweat and he's sitting forward again, clasping the front seat. His knuckles are stretched tight and his fingers burrow into the leather. I can feel the pulse in my neck twitch and my head's hurting so much, I can hardly keep my eyes open.

The guard makes a smart salute and opens the gate for us. The main compound is small. The ground is dust and, in it, are the tracks of a thousand boots. Further on, are three low, grey blocks with pitched roofs and bars at the windows. And over everything, curls of barbed wire are wound about like steel weeds. A watchtower to the left is occupied by a lone sniper but other than that and the guard, there's no one to be seen.

Beyond the blocks is a wide squat barracks with double doors at one end but no windows. I can hear the sound of machinery: a grinding and punching noise. My father turns to me. 'They're working. They make car batteries for export.'

'There are no windows,' I say.

He has an answer: 'No distractions.'

I feel myself gagging and I take a gulp of air. A cry from the building makes me jump. A solitary, animal scream that makes my teeth buzz, and then silence. Total silence. I look at him. He explains: 'Acid burns – from the batteries. It happens. They'll deal with it.'

The end of the compound is in sight and we reach the final building: a low, white block in three parts built around a kind of quadrangle. The windows are barred and boarded and the building itself surrounded by a barbed wire mesh that stands at least thirty feet high, the gates to which are chained and padlocked. A guard wearing a white surgical mask steps out, unlocks the gates and lets us through. My father motions me out of the car, and I follow him into the building in a trance.

Under the gaze of the guard, who looks bored, my father opens a tall cupboard at the back of the room. He selects two heavy packets wrapped in plastic from a large pile. He throws me one. 'Put this on please, Ben.' He goes on, as I take it: 'Ben, if I could go back, undo all I've done, don't you think I would do it in a heartbeat? All I can do now – all *we* can do – is to try to mitigate it.'

'It's OK.' But I don't know it is – I don't know anything anymore.

I tear open the pack and pull out a large rubberised body suit with a hood and visor. There's a pair of sterile boots and long fat gloves. I put the gear on, and my father does the same.. He nods to the guard, and I follow him through a set of doors into a long corridor with doors leading off it: sterile and dustless.

His eyes under the visor glitter. He puts a gloved hand on my shoulder, and I hear his breathing amplified inside his protective helmet. The heat is sinking into my skin. I'm drowning in it.

He turns, then paces away. His feet in their rubber boots squeak on the floor.

I'm about to say something more when a horn
sounds. I stand and peer through a high, thick window
across to the main prison block. And out of nowhere,
hordes of men in blue boiler suits emerge onto the
open ground of the main compound beyond our fence,
some running, some hobbling. Each carries a small
wooden bowl. On a command from a tannoy, they all
stand upright to attention with their arms at their side.
Another command comes and they sit, cross-legged
in the dust in rows. Flies cluster about their eyes and
mouths, and rest on their feeding bowls.

My father says, 'Meal time.'

A small cart is wheeled out. Two warders walk on
either side of it as it travels up and down the lines.
The men on the floor sit and wait, and as it stops, each
man shoots out a hand and something is ladled into his
bowl. They return the bowls to their laps and wait. The
whole process takes all of ten minutes, and, on a further
command from the tannoy, they dip their heads and eat,
scooping and pinching up the food in their hands. I see
a man whose face is swollen with bruises. All have their
heads shaved. All are thin, their faces hollow and wan.
And I wonder how I'm ever going to get out of here.

'How long?' I say through the visor.

He turns to me and it's almost as though he's
forgotten I'm there. The men are on the move again
and soon the square is quiet.

'Sorry?'

'How long will it take?'

'It's hard to say. There's a lot of work still to do. The sooner we get started the better.'

He punches in a code for a door at the end of the corridor and we go through it. We pass through two further doors and just inside the last is a thick plastic curtain that hangs in ribbons from the ceiling. The room is huge, cool and white. Large electric fans buzz overhead. But there's something about the air in the room: something rank and sour that I can't define but it curdles my stomach. Apart from the noise of the fans, the room is silent and at first, I think we're alone.

I'm wrong.

A little way up on the other side of the room, there's a small, glass internal cabin, locked and barred on the outside. Inside it, is a simple white hospital cot.

A man lies under a polythene tent. His hands claw at the plastic and his mouth hangs open. He's thin: his hip bones arch up and his ribs curve under tight yellow skin. The light inside the cabin is dim but I can see several dark swellings on his body.

My father turns to me. 'Ghastly accident. A few days ago he was caught trying to escape through the lab. He was exposed to the virus and contracted it within hours. There's nothing we can do – just try to keep him comfortable until the inevitable.'

I stare at the man but he looks right through me. My father says, 'He doesn't know where he is anymore. The fungus has taken over.'

'And there's nothing you can do?'

'Nothing. As soon as the vaccine is ready, I'll make sure all the men have it. But as I said, there is no cure for this.'

'And you injected this shit into me?'

He hangs his head.

I don't think I'm ever going to forget that face and the hands and their aimless groping. I'm still watching him when a short figure comes through a door at the end of the room. He too wears a rubberised suit.

My father looks up. 'This is Dr. Yeo. A colleague.'

Dr. Yeo peers up at me from inside his suit. His skin is spotted with little black moles.

'Pleased to meet you, Ben. Your father has told me a lot about you.'

They stand to one side and have a muted conversation, and I see the eyes of the man in the bed blaze. His heart pulses in his chest as he works to breathe.

Suddenly Dr. Yeo is standing next to me. 'This poor fellow's nearly at the end stage. We have been observing him. You see these growths: they're packed with spores. That's why he's under the tent. When they burst, they release thousands of spores, each of which will be busy looking for a host. You noticed him scratching at the tent? He wants to climb, wants to get up high. It's a feature of the parasite: makes the host want to get to the highest point, for maximum dispersal you see.'

My head's throbbing and I want to throw up.

My father calls me then. 'Ben! Come on! Come with me.'

He ushers me into the room from where Dr. Yeo had come. It's a small laboratory – microscopes, sterile chambers, test tubes and syringes. Around the walls are glass cages holding rats and monkeys; some lie listless in their straw, some scream and claw at the glass, their mouths open and drooling. All have huge black growths on their skin like the man in the tent. It's a little cooler in here although there are no fans.

He sees me check the ceiling. 'Air conditioning.' He points to a square white unit pumping in the corner. 'We need it so we can work.'

He sits, or rather slumps, onto a stool and looks at me. 'That man in there – what you just witnessed is horrible, I know. All I can say, all I can ever say, is that I'm trying to make amends. What I left for you to find may just do that. Rees will be exposed for what they really are, and if there's any justice in the world, they'll be ruined, wiped off the market. I would – I should – be in prison for what I've done but I hope that out here, I can actually go some way to preventing …'

My breath is steaming inside the visor. I'm not thinking straight. I lean back against the counter. My father gets up and walks to a door in the far wall of the small lab. He opens it and all I see is white.

He turns to me with the ghost of a smile. 'I think it's time we made a start.'

28

Press-ups, pull-ups, weights. The floor moving towards and away from me. Sweat on my back. Plastic, paper, rubber boots, stainless steel. The limits of my world: dark blood under glass – my blood – tubes and masks, and drifting in and out of consciousness.

The first month, under a full moon, two men escape. They'd cut through the wire with stolen pliers. One is brought back alive. I watch them haul him across the ground, his bare feet brushing up the dirt. Everyone is put on half rations for two weeks after that. They never found the other one. I like to think he made it.

Press-ups, pull-ups, weights. I can feel my body hardening from the inside out. We're a part of the place but we're not. The first Tuesday of every month Dad goes into Kunming for lab supplies. He's grown a beard that's way too big for his face. Once he brought me back a jar of boiled sweets that looked like eyeballs.

'I hope you like sweets,' he said. He put the jar down

carefully on the table in front of me, counting under his breath: 'One, one, one, two, two, two ...' And the sweets looked up at me. They were all the colours of the rainbow. 'They're all the colours of the rainbow,' he said, and he smiled with all his teeth and walked away before I could say anything.

Press-ups, pull-ups, weights. Six months. Half a year. Time here is like a kind of unfolding, an unravelling – until you're stretched like a skin drum and there's nothing to do but to roll yourself back up again and let the whole thing start over. I turned eighteen last week. I can do a hundred pull-ups in a row. And I can go without thinking about Sophy for a few hours. There seem to be fewer inmates here, although we have little or nothing to do with them.

Him and me, we're like two castaways, two souls in a boat at the edge of the world.

Press-ups, pull-ups, weights. Nine months. I've read books – books on bone density, blood disorders, on the life cycle of parasites. There's no Internet, nothing of or from the world outside. Dad never brings any news from Kunming. I read and I draw. I draw everything: snakes, butterflies, the prisoners standing in line at roll call, my father hunched over the counter in the lab, the bald prison guard with the missing teeth who brings us our food. I've started learning Mandarin. Sometimes I think I'm going mad. It's hard to keep a grip on reality when everyone around you is a prisoner in some way or another.

But every evening, when the sun goes down, there are two plastic chairs set in the same place with careful hands; one is turned to face the other at an angle. I look at Dad, and his eyes rest on the fences or the jungle behind and he talks about his work, his life, about Mum and Charlie, and the plans he kept close, too close. I'm learning to know him and it's not the same as *getting* to know someone. He's *teaching* me him, showing himself to me, bit by bit. He's still funny about food, still counts under his breath, and he's still pretty tough going in a conversation but sometimes in spite of it all, I can look at him and find what I thought I'd lost for ever.

One evening, when I've been there nearly ten months, he puts aside his plate and leans in. He sticks out a hand but curls it away from me before we touch. 'You look strong,' he says.

I look down along my arms and shrug. 'Maybe.'

'Like a film star,' he smiles. 'Yes, like a film star.' And he's off counting to himself.

'How much longer?' I say.

'We're close, you can go home soon.'

'And you? You can come too. Rees is finished – you know that. It was in the news when I left.'

'Mmm,' is all he says.

'What does that mean?'

He looks away and says, 'What will you do, Ben?'

'When we get home? Well, I'll … I don't know. Look for a job maybe? I could get my driving licence, drive a van or something.'

'I see.'

'*What?*'

'Well,' his hands tighten for a moment on the arms of his chair. 'I always think … I think you must *look* for your life. You won't find that driving a van.'

'I don't even know what that means.'

'It means that you must look at yourself – at what you want – and go in search of that, however hard it may be.'

I look at him.

'What do you want?' he says.

'I don't know.'

'Your pictures are very good. They are very good.' I smack at a mosquito on my arm and it bursts against my skin.

He goes on. 'I was thinking I would like to use one.'

'Yeah? How?'

'I'd like to give you a present. A tattoo. I know your mother wouldn't have approved but …'

'A tattoo? Are you serious?'

'Of course. The snake you drew. In China, it's a very … auspicious sign. It means new life, rebirth, healing, transformation. What do you think?'

'One of my drawings?'

He nods.

'Yeah,' I say, 'cool. Why not?'

'That's good. I am pleased.'

There's quiet for a moment then I say, 'So what will you do? When all this is finished?'

There's a long pause and the night closes around us. 'I've told so many lies, Ben. I've been a part of something so wicked, so ... profane. All I can ever do in my small corner of the world is to try to undo some of that.'

'You did some good too – the cancer stuff – you told me.'

'Not nearly enough,' he says slowly. 'Not nearly enough. The only goodness in my life came from your mother and Charlie and you – you were what helped me make sense of the world – and I wish to God that I could have let go of everything else and kept that. *I wish.*'

He pushes back his chair and walks away, and I hear his footfall faint against the jungle noise.

29

Today the tannoy is sounding when I come to.

Another procedure.

White light yawns through the window. Everywhere is white. It presses in on me like water. My arms prickle and pinch as I move and I see the blur of plastic tubing and red blood against the white. I close my eyes again.

I've been here nearly a year, and while most of the time, I can push away the past and home and everything, sometimes it just all gets to me – kind of explodes. Today is one of those days.

A door is opened and I hear footsteps but I don't open my eyes. A voice, my father's, is saying my name. 'Ben?'

With great effort I open my eyes and try to focus. A lean outline of a figure in white is standing over me. There's a sucking sound as a tube is pulled from my arm. A hot dry hand picks up mine. The palms are like leather. Like soft leather. But they smell of disinfectant. A needle is pressed into the back of my hand and I feel the fluid pulsing into me. For a while I'm hanging in limbo – waiting – reluctant to return but the fluid is relentless. It pushes through me into my head and my eyes and my heart, and at once I am fully awake. The whiteness leaches away and I can see colour and shape again. And my father is there, unmasked. His face is lined but he's smiling.

'Ben?'

I try to speak but instead my mouth bubbles and spits. I shake my head but I don't know what I'm responding to.

'Can you hear me? Ben?'

I try to lift my head and he lays a hand on my forehead. He turns then and says something to someone I can't see. Someone offers a glass of water. I take it and swill the liquid in my mouth but I can't swallow it. The water runs away down the corner of my mouth and I hear it spatter on the floor below.

Then a wave of nausea claims me and I gag and retch up bile. My arms are numb. I can hardly move. Besides my father, there are two other men in the room dressed in white scrubs. They stare at me. One of them is Dr Yeo, the other I don't recognise. I look up at my father and he says gently, 'It's over. Finished. We've done it. What you came here for. Can you wait outside for a moment, gentlemen?' and he leans in to me and says, 'This is a good day, Ben. The vaccine's ready. I'm proud of you. What you've done, what we've done together is a very good thing.'

'OK,' I say.

'You can go back to your life.' And he smiles. 'And because of you ... well ... But –'

'What is it?'

'What we talked about. Your snake. The tattoo.'

'Yeah?'

He calls to the others who come back in. 'This is Robert. He's going to give you the tattoo.'

'*Now?*'

I watch blinking as Robert steps up and pulls on a pair of plastic gloves.

'If that's all right,' says Dad and I nod. 'Can you turn over?' He hovers, his hands over my shoulders and helps me twist onto my front.

I'm face down on the trolley and I'm breathing in paper. Someone's hand is on my neck, hot and cold. I can hear his whispered counting and then he's saying to Robert, 'Yes ... the back, between the shoulder blades. Good, good idea. Here I think. It needs space. Here it is.'

I twist and crane my neck but all I see is white. Someone says something I don't catch and I hear the whistle of paper right behind me, then his breath, up close, in my ear: 'Hold still.'

His cold knuckles brush my cheek for a moment before he goes. Footsteps all around the trolley then a hand flat on my back, a smart wipe against the skin of something wet, then the rustle and stick of paper. Something is being traced on my back. Long lines and sharp points and loops. A ticking, then a whining like a dentist's drill and the needle comes down. Hot pricking and dragging against the skin, hands on me, holding me still. I close up. I look for Sophy.

It takes hours, and when it's done and the blood wiped away, they hold a mirror to show me. It's my design but altered: a cobra, rising out of its coils. It stretches up my back to my neck. The scales on its back are patterned green and blue and black, and its hooded eyes look out at the world over curved fangs and forked tongue.

30

Three days on, I'm shaken awake, pulled up roughly from my bed. Snatches of sunlight behind his silhouette and his bony fingers on me. The tattoo's still raw but healing, and there are points of blood on the sheet where I've lain.

'Ben! Get up! Wake up! Hurry!'

Something's different but I don't know what it is yet. And then I realise: it's the noise. The noises are different. I can't hear anyone. All I can hear is … something like machinery but far away. I don't recognise it.

His breathing is shallow. 'This is it, Ben. *Ben?* Time to go.'

'*Go?* Where? How can I just −?'

'Hurry please. I would say you have about five minutes.'

He wipes a run of spittle from the side of his mouth and looks behind him to the open door. '*Please?* Time is pressing. You have to go!'

I get up and I'm standing by the bed when he produces a package wrapped in plastic which he places on the bed. 'Open it. Clothes.' I do so and find a pair of jeans, trainers, a shirt and a jacket. He hovers near me while I dress. Then I see him reach into his jacket pocket. 'Here's some money – a thousand US dollars, and the passport you gave me. Get to Kunming, call this number. The money should be enough to get you home.'

He hands me a white business card curled at the edges. There's a number and a name on the card: MURRAY TREE.

'What? Who is this?'

He sighs and looks around him. 'A name. A man. He'll get you out, get you somewhere safe. Call him when you get to Kunming.'

'I don't understand. I don't need any help. I've got a passport, money, anyway, you'll be there. We can –'

He looks at me and I see him squeeze his hands into tight balls at his side. 'Things aren't what they were, Ben. Everything's changed. Trust me, you'll need help.'

I'm still trying to concentrate on what's happening here – to focus. It's like I'm standing still and everything around me is spinning. His face is pale and his breath comes in sharp barks. We stand facing each other, and I take the money and stare at it stupidly. 'What? What? What are you –?'

'They'll be here soon.'

'Who? Who'll be here soon? *For me?* Are they … is someone coming for me?'

A whirring, whirling noise makes us look up. Dark shadows at the windows and he turns to me with sad eyes. 'It's happened. What I hoped would never happen. I thought we were safe here, I thought we'd have more time. Time to get the stuff out. It's too late for that now.'

'*What? Too late for what?* What are *you* going to do?'

He walks towards me. I can hear voices, getting closer, and the clatter of gunfire. He pushes me through the door. 'There's no transport. You must walk up out of the valley to the ridge and keep heading south.'

'I'm not going without you.'

'I'll try to follow but –'

'What?'

'I can't let them get their hands on it. The fact they're here at all means they never finished it.'

'Finished what?'

'The vaccine,' he says. 'You *have* to go. I cannot – *will not* – let them take you.'

I can hear frenzied shouts and the sound of heavy boots on hard ground, and, far above, the chopping of helicopter blades. My father turns to the door. 'Just don't trust anyone. And … and don't tell anyone about you – about what you are – until you're safe.' There are tears in his eyes as he says it and he crooks his arm over his face to hide them. 'Ben, I am so very sorry for everything and so very, very proud of you.'

He shoves me towards the door. I can smell burning.

'No! You're coming with me!' I shout and I take his

arm and drag him through the outer room. He struggles but I'm stronger.

'Ben, *please*? No!'

The compound outside is full of men, some scaling the fences – the watchtower is empty – some squatting in the dust hiding their eyes, some huddled together looking up. A helicopter hangs in the sky overhead and whirs in the heavy air, churning up grit on the ground. I hear dogs barking. I turn to him and he squirms as I take his face in my hands. His eyes dart from side to side.

'Dad, I want you to come. I'm not leaving you.'

He nods, breathing hard. 'OK.'

He turns and runs with me at his heels, round to the back, away from the commotion. There's a small locked gate in the fence. He draws out a key chain and wrestles with the lock. He heaves it open and I go through. Behind us, the sound of dogs snapping and snarling, and ahead, a dirt track that cuts its way through the green. The air is steaming. I turn to take his arm but he's still in the compound, locking the gate behind me.

'*Dad?*' He spreads his fingers and pushes his hand against the wire onto mine. He's shaking his head. He looks into my eyes then, deep into them, a searching, loving look. I close my fingers on his, and his hand is warm.

'Dad, *please*? After all we've done? Please?'

'Go,' he says. 'Go and find your life. And whatever you see out there, whatever happens, try to think of me with kindness.'

He loosens his hand and steps back. His eyes are still on mine. Behind him, men are running in all directions, and now and again, there's a sharp burst of gunfire. I stand and watch him, his back square, his arms at his sides, walking away back to the lab.

He looks back once. He goes into the lab and closes the door behind him.

'Dad.' The word dries in my throat.

I can't see anymore and my fingers lock white against the wire. I can hear his counting in my head now: 'One, one, one, two, two, two, three, three, three …'

And all at once, from the lab there comes a splintering and a cracking like a thousand mirrors breaking, followed by a shower of bright flame and clouds of smoke that wheel and tower upwards.

I watch it burn down.

And inside it, as the glass shatters – his dark silhouette – arms raised and clawing at the sky, then falling and falling and falling into the flames.

I fold into shadow.

A helicopter sings in the crowded sky, and with tears in my eyes, I run.

Sophy, England, 2014

We're not supposed to go through the park anymore but I go anyway because a short cut is a short cut and it's so hard these days to just be on your own. I go past the bench by the swings and I remember that afternoon in the park a long time ago. That weird light you have in the sky — a grey brightness after the rain. The smell of rust and wet pavements, his thick hair over his face, his long limbs and how I wanted to kiss him, properly kiss him.

I'd never felt like that about a guy before. Never knew you could meet someone and know with all your heart that this person is so utterly, so perfectly right for you. And it wasn't because I felt sorry for him. It wasn't that at all. I can't explain it, except that when I saw him that first time across the street, it was like I'd found what I'd been looking for — what was missing.

And yes of course I got on with it. It wasn't like we were married or anything. But after he left, after he didn't come back, after I waited — it was like a door in the floor opened and I just fell through it. Like Alice in Wonderland or something.

And yes, I can come back through; until it got really bad, I was planning a gap year in America with Amy. But most of the time, I'm sort of stuck there and you know what's weird? I'm still waiting.

His brother came to see me a while after it happened. It's stupid how I keep saying after 'it happened' because nothing did happen. No news, no plane crash, no tsunami. Nothing. It's just like one day there was no Ben and there just wasn't going to be. Anyway, like I said, Charlie came to see me. And he was so like him, standing on the doorstep, that it hurt behind my eyes to see him.

He sat in the front room with his hands between his knees and he said nothing. Just looked at the carpet. For ages. And I sat opposite him and when he looked up, his eyes were wet. And I went across to him and we held each other. The smell of soap and the raw husk of his uniform against my cheek.

They were sending him away. But when I asked him about Ben, he had nothing to say – only that he'd told him, he'd warned him – and how he should have stopped him.

I wrote letters, emails. I was even in touch with someone who worked at Rees. Nothing.

Nothing.

Until today.

I'm woken up by my phone buzzing by my bed. The networks are down so often that getting a call is always a surprise. I fumble for it and it jumps away from me, thrumming. The screen shows: 'Unknown Caller'.

When I answer it there's a long airy wait. Just thin crackles of static. And then a voice, far away, thin and broken – a girl: 'You Ben friend?'

Needles prickle my skin. I pull my knees up to my chest and stare at the phone. For what seems like ages I can't answer. And then I say, 'Yes, Yes! Is he there? Is he OK? Is he alive?'

Another wait while the wind sings in the line and then, 'He's alive.'

'Oh my God! Is he there? With you? Can I speak to him? Please?'

'No. He not here.'

'Where? Where is he? When can I … How can I …?'

Hot tears on my face.

There's a pause. 'I don't know. I see Ben and he give me number and he say to me call you.'

'When? When did you see him?'

I'm shouting and her tone changes. It's sharper now. 'I have to go.'

And I ask because I have to ask because I have to know. I spit the words out in a tight breath. 'Is he … is he sick? Has he—?'

'Sick? Maybe sick. Don't know. I have to go.'

And the walls of my room shrink and I'm curled inside them: me and this girl from the other side of the world. I jump then and ask what I should have asked before.

'Where are you? In China? Is he still in China? Are you in China now?'

But I know the line is dead. Even as I'm speaking I know it's dead.

The seven o'clock siren sounds. Dawn is breaking, a rosy blush in the sky over the rooftops. On the bed the phone is cold in my hand.

THE END

A NOTE ABOUT THIS BOOK

My father was a military scientist. In the 1980's, he was working on top-secret defence projects.

Back in January 1987, when I was a young woman, I came home from work to hear that my father had died. There were no details at that point.

I got a lift to my parents' house – about an hour's journey – and it was then, many hours after his death, that I found out what had happened.

My father had appeared to leave for work early, and my brother, 16 years old at the time, had gone down later to make breakfast.

He heard the car engine running in the garage. When he went out, the garage door was shut.

He went to investigate but it was too late. My father was dead.

It looked like a straightforward suicide – carbon monoxide poisoning. But later on, as the days and weeks passed, and journalists started calling, we began to understand that others like him had died in suspicious circumstances. Between 1987 and 1988, at least twelve scientists and computer experts working in Britain's high-tech defence industry had died in bizarre, often grisly ways. Questions were asked in parliament and the press but the government dismissed calls for an enquiry.

I don't know what really happened, why my father died, or whether there is a mystery to solve, but I suppose, writing this book, and beginning it the way I did, is in part, about me looking for my father as Ben does for his.

I hope you enjoy it. And if you do, please leave a review on Amazon or your e-platform of choice.

ACKNOWLEDGMENTS

Writing Bad Blood was a lot of fun. Most of the time. When it wasn't and I got stuck, my lovely family were always there with ideas and support and snuggles. They've taken me out for drinks, picked me up off the floor, reassured me, given me confidence, kept me going. I want to thank them all: TB for his loving kindness at every turn – and for reading it! Mouse for the amazing conversations and wild-geese; Roo, for his incisive editing; and Stewie, for her belief that one day this would be a book.

I want to thank others too: My dear stepsons; the fabulous Dr Steve Conway (Stevie Wonder) for his very patient tutorial on antibiotics; my super friend Julia, for her A level biology sessions; to Sara Starbuck for her positive energy; to my partner-in-crime and superbly, fiendishly, wonderful editor, Lisa; to Mike for the amazing cover design; and to Jane Conway for all the coffee and buns.

Thank you.

This is one of two. And yes, I know I've left you hanging a little, but Part Two is in the pipeline and will be out on bookshelves very soon.

COMING SOON FROM JANE BRITTAN:

BAD BLOOD
PART TWO

'They're infected,' he says, 'Late stage.
They live on the motorways. That's what
the tank patrols are for.'

The thrilling sequel to Bad Blood is told by both Ben and Sophy, thousands of miles apart. The UK is in the grip of a terrifying epidemic and Ben is stranded half way across the world. Somehow he must make it back to the West, to freedom, to Sophy, and to do what he was made to do.

There's a taste in my mouth like sour sweat. Like someone else's sweat. Like I've just leaned in and licked it up from someone's neck. And no matter how much I swallow it stays there. On my tongue and around my teeth. The air is heavy like water.

I've been going in circles.

I headed upwards out of the valley to the ridge like he told me. It took me hours. Clawing my way through tree roots and scree. Toe by toe. Once the whirling blade of a helicopter clipped the dark canopy above me scattering a shower of bright creepers and branches and a caterwaul of angry shrieks of birds or animals from the treetops.

I reached the ridge at night fall. Noises from the valley below carried up in the steaming air. Urgent cries, panic, gunshots. I lay back on flat ground and closed my eyes feeling the earth humming and turning under me. I lay there for a few minutes and when I opened my eyes it was dark. A thick black breathing darkness that pricked at my eyes and my skin.

The climb finished me. Every muscle in my body trembled and my head hurt like hell but I knew I should keep moving, force myself to get up and push through the binding vines and tree trunks to find the track we came in on. Then, done for, I rolled myself away from the lip of the valley and pitched myself into a shallow dip in the forest floor.

That was yesterday. The heat wakes me. Sharp and close. I shuck off my jacket and push myself up on my elbows. My skin is blistered with insect bites and sweat's pooling at my neck and waist. It's quiet in the valley now and when I look down there's thin black plumes of smoke from far below. They must have torched the place.

The sun is high in the sky before I get going again. Standing up is hard enough but walking kills me. My legs feel sore and brittle; muscles in my back and knees snap and tick as I move. I stay high up and head west looking for the dirt track in the green.

But the undergrowth here is so dense it's all you can do just to shoulder your way through it. It twists and weaves away from you until before you know it, you're facing the way you've come. Running is impossible. It's knitted itself together and you can't break it. All you can do is work your way around it. Slowly. Cutting and teasing the whiskery vines: lifting them over my head while all around me the jungle grubs and calls and scratches.

To move forward at any speed, I have to dip down and so lose the ridge line. Without it I can't see the track. By dusk on the second day I'm so lost I can't tell which is up or down. And I need water. I can feel my insides drying; sucking in away from my skin; contracting. Even standing still I can feel my pulse driving. I spend what feels like a lifetime trying to lap water from a thin runnel on a branch but the effort of it is too much and the lick of brackish water on my tongue makes me retch and gag.

I'm going in circles.

I know I should spend the night off the ground but I just can't get it together. I lie where I fall and close my eyes.

I'm going in circles.

I must have slept because a cramp in my leg wakes me and I'm rubbing and pulling at my calf when I hear it. The sound of breathing: shallow and choky. It stops after a minute and I wait. I wait and my breath stops in my chest. And I know before I know that there's someone else out here. Close. Close enough to smell him. Something different. Chemical maybe. Whatever it is it doesn't belong out here.

Like me.